When sixteen-year old Valerie Trumble leaves Suburban Etobicoke for the bright lights of Toronto, she soon discovers that there are things much worse than wooden beaver wallpaper or her mother's 'gross' cooking. Now, with only a black leather jacket and two hockey bags full of clothing, she must fend for herself in the big, bad city.

Fortunately, this is the early eighties, and the punk scene is large and vibrant. Valerie soon finds accommodations at the Terrible House of Sickness, the most notorious punk house in town. Glue-sniffing skinheads, drunken bikers, and hamster-gargling punk rockers are only a few of the things she must learn to live with. What will become of little Valerie Trumble? Will her dignity survive in this harsh environment? Or is she destined to become just another burnt-out casualty of the streets?

Take a trip back in time to the halcyon days of punk, to Queen Street and Kensington Market, where the nights are long and the party never ends.

Spunk Punkette Seeks Adventure and Romance

A Novel of Punk Rock Toronto in the 1980s C.E.

Second Edition

Including

The End of the Human Race

A "Bonus Track" Science Fiction Short Story not included in the First Edition

Author: Stewart Black

Spunky Punkette Seeks Adventure and Romance originally published as part of the *Double A-Side* double novel *Destroy Canada* in 2005 c.e. An C by GFY Books Vancouver, British Columbia.

Spunky Punkette Seeks adventure and Romance editted by Chris Walter of GFY Books

Back cover blurb courtesy of Chris Walter of GFY Books

Photograph of Author courtesy of Sharny Nicoloff (Sharon Cameron)

Special thanks to Chris Walter of GFY Books

ISBN 978-0-244-74574-5

This book is dedicated to everybody who was on the Toronto scene from the Time of the Diodes to the era of the Bunchofuckingoofs.

Chapter One

I hate it when people are always asking me why I left home when I was sixteen. I usually just say there's no law against it, but because people are so nosy they go on asking me what the real reason was, and if I don't think they'll take it back to some social worker or my mother, I tell them it's because I hated it at home. My mother is still going around telling all her friends and the people she works with at the glass factory, and everybody else that'll listen to her story, that she doesn't understand why I left. I bet she does it with a shrug. She'll tell them that she did her best to make it a happy home and act like she's the victim because she was, oh, such a good mother. But when you look at it, it was only a happy home for her.

I hated her food. There was lots of boiled cabbage and cheap beef or pork chops every night, and it was boring and made me feel heavy. Every time I got up from the table, I felt nailed down under that load of greasy food. And as for the vegetables... Yeah, I had the choice about whether or not I wanted to butter the cabbage, but that wasn't the point. I know I've got to eat vegetables or get sick, but I couldn't stand the cabbage, cabbage, cabbage, five or six times a week or maybe those over- cooked peas, carrots and cauliflower boiled twenty-five minutes. Can you believe that? Twenty-five minutes! That's murdering the vita-mins. So it's like food, but it's not food--it's what's left of food when the nutritious part has been boiled out, food that's been turned to shit even before the stomach and intestines had a chance to turn it to shit. That shit was on my plate every night, and there was no talk at the table but her nagging me to eat that shit.

I'd say, "Mom, I'm sick of eating these same things every night. Can I skip dinner just this once? Please?"

And she'd sigh and look up at the ceiling in disgust and roll her eyes around and then look back at me and say, "Valerie shut up and eat your cabbage and pork chops before you let them go cold."

But the food wasn't shit to her because she liked it. Brad liked it too. He's her live in boyfriend. I would have preferred carrot sticks or celery sticks with a bit of mayonnaise to dip it in on the side, but there was no mayo, and one night when I asked for it, she said, "Valerie, we're not having bar food in this house."

I said, "How the hell am I supposed to know what's bar food and what's not? I'm only fourteen. I'm not the one who comes home half plastered every couple of weeks, am I?"

Then she got real mad and we had a fight because I said the word 'hell', and I said, "It doesn't matter because you say it often enough yourself."

Then she looked at the ceiling again and muttered, "Heaven help me! Heaven help me!"

I ate the pork chops that night, just to shut her up, even though I hated them. Then I went to the toilet and stuck my finger down my throat and threw them up because they were making me feel so heavy and gross. Later when I was coming in from the porch, I overheard her saying to Brad that she wished she had the money to send me to a shrink because she heard me puke and was sure I was going bulimic. She thought I didn't hear, and I wanted to scream in her face, "I'm not crazy. It's just that your food is shit!"

But I didn't, of course. I was so mad that I had to lock myself in my room and I couldn't think of anything else all night. I couldn't even sleep.

And how about the furniture in that house? I hated that too. All those blow torched end tables and bookends that look like antiques but aren't antiques? Fuck, I hate fake things. Fake things are for fake people. Every tabletop, counter or otherwise useful space was covered with those ugly wooden beavers. I think that Canadian patriotism is fine, but there are limits. My mother covered the kitchen with beaver wallpaper too. Not just pictures of beavers, but wouldn't you know it, wooden beavers! My mother found wallpaper with a wooden beaver pattern!

The day after I threw up the pork chops, she and Brad came back from the mall with the new rolls of wallpaper and she said, "Valerie, we're going to wallpaper the kitchen. Do you think you could help?"

I said, "Yeah," because it was something to do, and she never usually asked me to help with anything.

Brad was looking pretty smug with his new painter's cap and carrying the rolls of paper and the paste. He didn't say much as usual because he never says much in front of her, except maybe, "Yes, dear."

I thought that wallpapering over the old pattern and getting rid of the fuckin' beavers was a great idea. If I had to eat cabbage, at least I wouldn't have to feel sick looking at wooden beavers on the wall, but when we unrolled the first roll, it was another pattern of wooden beavers! Only these were worse because they were bigger and had smiles on them and big eyes that bugged out as if they were looking at you.

I said, "There's no way I'm putting more beavers up. I'm sick of beavers. They're all over the house."

And she said, "Now Valerie, you'll get used to them," in a voice like she was teasing me. But she wasn't teasing, she was tormenting. I could tell by her sadistic tone.

"I hate the beavers," I said. "Put the wallpaper up yourself," and walked off.

But she said, "Valerie, you get back here this minute. Who do you think you are to talk to me in that tone of voice?"

I came back to the kitchen and said, "What do you mean? You were the one being sarcastic 'cause you know I hate beavers."

"You're paranoid."

"There you go talking as if I'm crazy again. Just like you did last night when you told Brad I should see a shrink because you think I'm going bulimic."

She said, "How dare you snoop in on my conversations!"

I said, "Snoop? I heard it loud and clear when I came in the house from the porch. I'm not a snoop like you. I can't even have a normal phone life because if anybody calls me from school, you're listening in on the other line. You're the snoop, mother. I don't know what you're checking up on when you listen in on those phone calls. I don't have a boyfriend, I'm not pregnant, and I'm not crazy! I just hate pork chops. They make me feel heavy and sick! I told you that before and you didn't listen. You never listen!"

All this time Brad was at the sink, stirring the paste with an old bit of hockey stick and acting like this conversation wasn't going on, and I hated him. Then he said, "Dear, forget her. Let's just get the wallpaper up."

Mom didn't listen to Brad, but went on to yell, "You little ingrate, you don't appreciate the price of a pork chop. Wait till you start working. Then you'll know how much these things cost. And there's nothing wrong with the beavers. They make the house look pretty. Further, I'm not a snoop, and I'll tell you another thing Valerie. When you leave home you can decorate your house however you please, but don't tell me how to decorate mine!"

I yelled, "That's all right with me because you won't be invited, and besides, I'm going to leave home when I'm sixteen and there is no law against it!" Then I added, "And I won't ever buy a pork chop because I hate them! That's all. I'm not saying they aren't expensive!"

She laughed at me and said, "You're not leaving home till you're at least twenty, Valerie. So stop giving me this crap and get used to living with the beavers 'cause that's the way it's going to be."

Then I walked out of the room. She screamed, "Get the hell back in here. I haven't finished talking to you!"

I came back even though I didn't want to. She yelled some more about something that I can't remember now and then she slapped me. I just ran out crying and I could hear Brad trying to calm her down by calling her 'dear' and trying to get her to focus on the wallpaper again.

•••

Well that fight was bad enough, but it got worse. Much worse. She and Brad had a couple of rolls left over, so they did half a wall in the bathroom. I couldn't even sit on the crapper without those stupid wooden beavers staring back at me with their weird, lecherous smiles unless I closed my eyes and imagined that I was somewhere else.

And there was another thing that was bugging me. It was the sex. Not like I was getting any, I wasn't even fifteen, but it bugged me that she kept on joking by saying things like, "Valerie, you be in the house by nine, or else. Brad and I don't want you getting pregnant or something."

I said nothing and tried hard not to make a face so she wouldn't see how fuckin' humili-ated I felt.

Shit, it wasn't like I had a boyfriend or anything. I just didn't want her joking about my sexuality. The teachers in sex education tell you at school that you shouldn't let anybody belittle you. That means that if you're a teenage girl, and a strange woman comes up to you on the street and says you're a little slut for the clothes you wear, or a pervert says something, just give the asshole a piece of your mind and get the hell out of there. Why did I take this harassment from my family? Why do some people think the rules stop at home? Meanwhile she and Brad fucked in the back bedroom any time they felt like it, futon frame creaking in time to Elvis's *Love Me Tender* blaring on the cassette deck.

Other things bugged me too. It wasn't just cabbage, sex, beavers and bitching. Some-times on the weekend when Brad was chilling out from his job working on the roads all day, he'd sit back in the living room chair with his can of beer in his hand listening to some shit like Elvis or the Beatles on the oldies radio station and say, "It ain't perfect, but sometimes on a quiet afternoon like this, this house is our own little bit of heaven."

I wanted to scream! Yeah, it's perfect, perfect for who? The two of them had the food they liked, the decor they liked, the music they liked and their own little sex nest. And quiet? With Elvis blaring? Please, I like punk rock: the Pistols, Clash, and Ramones, because punk is the only music intelligent enough to come right out and say that there's something fuckin' wrong with this world!

I wasn't allowed to play my music on the stereo if anyone had a headache, or would rather have silence or be listening to something they liked. But that's not the reason I left home. The clothes drove me out. On my own time, I could wear punk rock T-shirts with logos like the Misfits, Forgotten Rebels or The

Young Lions on them, and my jeans ripped at the knee, that was no problem, but when I went to school, I had to wear these stupid looking polo shirts and other prissy things. They weren't even real polo shirts, but shitty imitations of brands like Lacoste. I almost barfed when I looked at myself in the mirror. Nobody at school dressed that way. T-shirts and jeans without holes are alright, I guess, but polo shirts are stupid looking things that only teachers and school council nerds wear. It's not as if Prince Charles or some member of the Royal Family is going to see you wearing one here in Etobicoke, the lamest suburb of Toronto, and invite you to join his polo team to play against the king of Sweden. Only a teacher could think stuff like that looks casual or professional.

And what about mom and Brad? They dressed like slobs. They were such horrible slobs that you'd be embarrassed to walk into a dough-nut shop with them. Them, with their beer stained ski jackets, old T-shirts and jeans almost worn through.

Brad should have known better and stood up for me because my mother at least listened to him sometimes, but he didn't. He had his hair down to his ass despite the fact that he was pushing forty. I say he should have known better, because his mother had bitched and nagged him about his long hair when he was my age. He had never cut it to a decent length 'cause all that bitching had given him a complex. Despite all that, he didn't leave home until he was thirty. Here he was pushing forty, and still rebelling against something he had never rebelled against properly, listening to the same shit music he listened to at fourteen. He probably thought I would put up with all the harassment just because he had.

Well I'm not so spineless. When you're fifteen, your clothes are your own business. It's just an invasion of privacy to tell someone what to wear, especially when you're no good example yourself. I told them, I told them, and I told them, ever since I was fourteen. They should have paid attention, but they didn't. They just laughed.

I said, "I'm leaving on my sixteenth birthday! There's no law against it, and there's nothing you can do about it!"

They laughed at me, but I kept saying it. I rubbed it into Brad's face, that although he stayed home until he was thirty, I would be mature enough to leave home by the time I was sixteen. He laughed at me as if I was still nine years old, but on my sixteenth birthday I had my bags packed and I was at the door. I stood there in my black leather jacket with the big studded collar, ripped jeans and Dead Boys T-shirt full of safety pins. My bleach blond hair stood twelve inches straight up in hard spikes because I had filled it with a whole bar of soap and blow-dried it. Fully transformed, I looked like the girlfriend of GBH, the punk band with the biggest mohawks. I said, "I told you, I told you, I told you! There's no law against me going, and never talk to me again!" I had a taxi outside to take me far away from them.

Then I walked out that door, with mom and Brad screaming and crying as if they were the fuckin' victims.

Chapter Two

Without looking back at my mother and Brad on the porch, I threw my two hockey bags of stuff into the taxi, jumped in and said, "Kipling Subway." I tried to sound adult, but I heard a lilt in my voice, and I must have sounded just like a little girl.

The driver didn't notice. He said, "Yep," and we sped away.

For a moment, I thought he was going to ask me why I wasn't with my mother or some-thing like that. Stupid paranoia, I guess, but he didn't ask, so I crossed my legs and looked at my nails. I wanted to give the impression I was used to ordering taxis even though this was my first time.

The taxi stopped by the buses outside Kipling Station and the driver said, "That's fifteen bucks forty cents."

I dug into the pocket of my leather jacket and paid him. It hurt to part with that much money, but it was worth it to make a clean get-away. The taxi pulled away and the driver yelled out the window, "No tip! Fuck you, you fuckin' punk rock piece of shit!"

That pissed me off, and I had my first adult realization. I realized that the world is full of stupid name-calling nothings; people who don't grow up, just like high school. That kind of thing is scary to know once you're on your own.

I went into the station and waited on the platform. I was sitting on the bench, when I heard a woman's voice as she walked down the stairs. It sounded like my mother talking to Brad.

"Shit!" I said.

I jumped behind a pillar, and I could still hear the woman's voice. She came to the bottom of the stairs, and I could see it was just the cleaning lady talking to herself, but the incident had spooked me, and I stayed behind the pillar and watched the stairs. I started thinking that the cab driver had been so pissed off with me for not tipping that he phoned my mother and now he was bringing her here to get me. It was probably his standard mean trick to play on sixteen-year-olds who were trying to leave home but didn't tip. The second hand on the fuckin' clock on the platform wasn't even fuckin' moving, and ten minutes felt more like ten hours before the train finally came.

I got on and threw my bags onto a seat. We were at the end of the line, so it took another five minutes for the train to leave the platform. It seemed like ten hours, and I sat on the train watching the stairs in case my mother came down. When the doors closed, I shut my eyes, sat back and breathed deep. I realized all those thoughts about the taxi driver and my mom were just paranoia.

I got off at Spadina Station. From there I hopped on a bus south to Kensington Market, near Chinatown. I got off at Dundas and went right into the streets of the market until I found the alley I was looking for. It was behind a Vietnamese restaurant and a used clothing store that sold some really fuckin' cool red leather belts with three rows of studs in them. At the back of the alley was a stairway, one of those metal fire escape jobs. It went up to a second floor that used to be part of a warehouse. One window and a big metal door set in chipped red bricks. The stairway was covered in old bicycle parts, mostly chains and rims. Dogs, big German Shepherds, three of them, were tied up on the top level. All three had studded black leather collars that looked as if they had been ripped off the backs of the bikers in that Mad Max movie. They started barking when they saw me. I climbed to the top, and they started growling. I could see a little ways inside the door, but there was only darkness. I yelled out, "I want to talk to Steve! Is there anybody home?"

A voice yelled out, "Come in! Just walk by the dogs. They won't bite."

I walked past, and the dogs barked and growled as if they wanted to eat me. I stayed as far away from them as I could by hugging the railing and jumping through the door. Then I was in a beat up kitchen. The yellow linoleum was worn out, and the fridge and walls were spray-painted with so much graffiti that it was too cluttered to read. Boxes of empty beer bottles took up a whole side of the room.

I walked through the door at the other end. It looked as if it had been a living room, but everything was spray-painted just like the kitchen. There was a big black Pearl drum kit with double bass drums in the middle of the floor. Against the walls, there were two huge stacks of Marshall amps and a mixing board. I could also see a couple of beat up guitar cases covered in hardcore punk stickers, a red and black Fender Precision Bass, a blood coloured Gibson guitar and a microphone stand. I thought *fuckin' eh! I'm in the practice spot of Sickness!* I knew it really was their space because Sickness was the only punk band that used double bass drums. Those drums made their music sound so driving and aggressive that you would think a truck was coming through the wall.

In front of the drums, in his black leather jacket covered in bike chains and red anarchist slogans, was Steve Sickness. He was the only one home, and he was sitting back on an old sofa sipping a Black Label beer. His black and red mohawk with the goatee beard was so fuckin' cool.

I went up to him and said, "Steve, do you remember me, Valerie?"

He put his beer down, looked my way and said, "Of course I do. I bump into you about once a month at the Record Peddler, and we talk. You're all fuckin' punked out, I see. You don't look like some suburban kid no more."

He pointed to my bleached, spiked hair. I was so fuckin' flattered that he noticed, and I was so fuckin' happy that he remembered me. I said, "Yeah, that's right."

He moved over to make room on the sofa and said, "Yeah, you must be our number one fan. You talk about our record all the time, even though you've never been to a show. You're the only person who thought the record was great. Every punk in Toronto said it sucked because we're much better live."

I said, "Steve, you told me I could live here for a while if I wanted."

He put his army boots up on the guitar amp in front of the table and said, "Yeah, as long as you're over sixteen. I can't have the cops coming in with a warrant to charge me with harbouring runaways."

"I know. Today's my sixteenth birthday."

"Congratulations."

"I told my family, my mom and her boyfriend Brad, to fuck off and never talk to me again. I hate them. I left today and there's no fuckin' way I'm going back. Steve, I just got to fuckin' stay here at the Terrible House of Sickness! There's no fuckin' way I'm going to one of those group homes for kids with difficult family backgrounds. No fuckin' way! My friend Susan from high school lived in one for a while and told me all about it. You have to go through regular counselling which is worse than school or parents. And the worst is that they use those places as halfway houses for juvenile delin-quents and young adult offenders. They put you on the same level as fuckin' criminals just for having problems at home. If I went there, I'd get my stuff stolen and get beat up again and again! I don't want to live in one of those fuckin' places and get raped. Fuck, even guys get raped in places like that. All I want is some place to live and have fun."

But Steve just sipped his Red Label and looked up at the ceiling.

I said, "Well I want to fuckin' live here! Is it fuckin' OK or not?"

"I already said you could, just as long as you got twenty bucks a week, don't eat anybody else's food, don't tell anybody how to live, and help sell the beer at night. This place doubles as a boozecan, you know."

I was so fuckin' happy. I said, "Yes! Yes! Yes!"

He gave me a beer, and we sat on the broken sofa in the rehearsal room. He let some of the dogs in and they sat around us sniffing each other's asses. They had stopped growling at me, and I felt accepted. I told Steve all about the fuckin' pork chops I hated, and he told me how dogs taught him how to live and why they only sold Black Label at the boozecan. All Toronto punks drink that brand because Steve Leckie of the Viletones drank it back in the glory days of '77 when punk was born and Sire Records gave him a record deal. No rocker would touch the stuff.

First thing I did after I got to stay at the Terrible House was call school and tell them to fuck off. Not like I'd gone much in the last year anyway.

The Terrible House was a place where punks, dozens of them, lived and partied. There were all sorts of punks with hair cut with razor blades and dyed blue or green. All the coolest had mohawks that stuck up in big jags set with hairspray and soap. Everybody had a black leather jacket with an A in a circle spray painted on the back or a Direct Action band patch tacked on with safety pins.

Real life punks have to live together to stay alive. They have to avoid so-called 'normal' people. They have to tell those people to fuck off the second they start trying to tell them what clothes they should be wearing. I mean this was 1981 -- there were what, a couple hundred punks in Toronto? There were hundreds of thousands of normalisms wearing the same fuckin' clothes and listening to the same fuckin' music in this city. There were billions of other mindless robot normalisms all round the world doing the same fuckin' thing. How the fuck is it that people like that can't put enough logic together to figure out that a few punks are not a threat to their way of life? How much of an asshole do you have to be to think you're fuckin' somebody special if you take a fuckin' unpro-voked swing at the underdog?

The Terrible House of Sickness was the party palace I always dreamed of. I slept on the floor or sofa or anywhere the empty bottles hadn't piled up or the dogs weren't sleeping. Besides the guys in the band, Steve, Ringo, Crushed-Nuts, and Bumper, I lived with a bunch of girls who were something like Sickness groupies. Those girls were always changing; one would move in one week and out the next. I remember the main girls. There was Bambi who was straggly like a rat, but always had her mohawk soaped up so it stood in spikes. She always wore a dirty ballerina skirt under her long black leather jacket. There was Melanie with the rotten teeth who always wore dirty, torn sweaters kept together with huge safety pins. There was Regan who had long black hair and ten big silver skull rings on her fingers. She always dressed in black funeral dresses like Morticia from the Adams family, and was so beautiful she could have been a model. There was Dog, who never said much, but was fat, had short hair and punched the walls a lot. I think she only had one pair of torn jeans and one T-shirt. Then, of course, there was me - Valerie.

There was nothing to do all day but sit around, listen to the Damned and the Buzz-cocks, pass around a joint, have a beer or just catch up on gossip about what other punks were doing and what gigs were coming up. There was no mom, no Brad, and no school. There was just punk rock and my part-time job. I used to work at Burger King in Etobicoke, but I arranged to have myself transferred to downtown Toronto as soon as Steve let me move in.

One afternoon the girls at the house dyed their hair green or got a mohawk or both. I dyed my hair green, but left it long, halfway to my ass. It looked fuckin' great against my black leather jacket with its chrome studs and wide lapels. At work, I tucked my hair up inside my cap. I was lucky that my manager understood, but she told me to stay in the kitchen and out of sight of the customers. She also said I couldn't be promoted to counter staff unless I dyed it back to its original colour. That was fine with me; it's not as if it was my life's ambition to be promoted to counter staff at a fuckin' Burger King!

After a couple of weeks, me, Bambi, and Dog tried to put together an all-girl Sickness tribute band called Morning Sickness. Bambi even designed a logo with a silhouette of a cute punkette barfing on the Toronto skyline. I was supposed to play drums. We assumed that Sickness would feel complimented and that we could use their equipment. I went out and bought some sticks from Long and McQuade down on Bloor Street and Spadina, but Ringo, the drummer, told me he'd punch my head if he ever caught me touching his kit, and so we never got it together. Ringo was the nicest guy, but you never could be quite sure about him. He had this habit of breaking an entire house with his head whenever he got drunk. It was too bad that we couldn't use their equipment. In Toronto, every punk you meet is in a band. Just goes to show you how much energy punks have, and how little creativity fuckin' normal-isms have.

Bambi and Dog kept dreaming about getting a band together and wouldn't stop talking about it. Bambi said that if we couldn't be a band, we could be a gang. She had big patches of the logo printed. We all sewed these to the back of our leather jackets and soon everybody was calling us the Morning Sickness Girls or the Puking Punkettes, and getting out of our way as if we were dangerous, even the other punks. It was cool to hear people call us names like Melanie Morning Sickness or Dog Morning Sickness. And that's how I got my punk rock name, Valerie Morning Sickness. It sounded so much better than Valerie Trumbel, and made me feel like a new person, like I had divorced myself from my fuckin' mom by not sharing her name no more. I was no longer 'Valerie Trumbel who hates her fuckin' pork chops,' I was 'Valerie Morning Sickness, get the fuck out of my way or you'll get your fuckin' head broken!'

Everybody came over to the Terrible House of Sickness to buy beer and get drunk after the bars shut. That's what a Toronto booze-can is -- a party place where you can buy beer under the counter when the bars close. For the most part, it was just talking about everything and listening to the Ramones and

Motorhead all night. But sometimes there were fights 'cause Ringo, the drummer, used to get stupid and break people's heads when he was on PCP. That was OK because he was the drummer, and we all expected it. Drummers are just like that.

Overall, there was a lot less violence than at some fuckin' suburban rocker party, because Toronto rockers can't drink two beers without starting a fight.

If Steve wasn't too drunk he'd fuck girls in the cage around his bed. He used to lock the girls in there if he liked them. I never had sex with the band because I was afraid of diseases. I was safe from sexual predators because I was a Morning Sickness Girl. The band would have kicked the shit out of anybody who bothered me.

One night some longhaired idiot who played guitar for a Led Zeppelin tribute band called Whole Lotta Led and who looked like a skinny version of David Lee Roth from Van Halen came over. He was welcome because he was an old friend of Steve's. Later he got drunk and tried to push me into a closet and pull my clothes off. I kicked him so hard in the nuts that they had to call an ambulance. Nobody was pissed off at me, even though we had to break up the party before the police came. I did what I had to do in self-defence, right? Steve even apologized to me and gave the guy a shot in the head before the medics showed up. That was cool of him.

And the fun never stopped! All I had to do on top of paying twenty dollars a week was help sell the beer so the band could pay their rent. I met everybody on the scene. Nazi Dog, Steve Leckie, came over and showed me his arms full of skeleton tattoos and knife scars. I talked all night with Rob from Youth Youth Youth about how he dyed his hair like a brown and blond checkerboard. One night DOA crashed at the Terrible House after driving across Canada, and Joey Shithead spent the night telling me how the Toronto clubs like Larry's and the Turning Point sucked compared to the Smilin' Buddha in Vancouver. I told Joe I'd come and visit him as soon as I got the cash together for the bus ride, but I never did.

Most of my money went on rent and beer. The problem was that food was expensive because I had to buy it from the convenience store. There was no stove -- Ringo had busted it with his head -- and the only good burner was used for hot knifing hashish. I couldn't use the fridge to store anything because it was always full of beer. I got to feeling low on energy some-times, but every night the beer and benzedrine tablets got me going, and life was a party again.

Melanie and Dog were the greatest girls to hang out with because they had a great sense of humour for mean practical jokes. One time we paid three dollars for a twenty-five-word ad in the Personal page of the Classifieds in NOW Magazine, Toronto's wimpy entertainment rag. We wanted to humiliate some of the lame ass guys on the punk scene. It read:

Spunky Punkette Seeks Romance and Adventure:
Oi! Cute punkette seeks punk guy for up and down 'pogoing' and a slam dance in the sack. Send photo to PO Box: 3277223

We got a bunch of pictures of stupid Italian guys standing next to Trans Ams showing off their moustaches and flexing their muscles. They wrote stupid shit like, "I may not look punk, but I'm punk inside. I am stacked like you need, baby!" We had lots of fun laughing at those idiots, but the funniest res-ponse we got was from Peter the part-time punk from the suburb of Scarborough who used to come to the Terrible House to party every Saturday. He sent us this fuckin' picture of himself with his hair spiked up and his dick hanging out. He looked so fuckin' stupid that Melanie and me made a hundred big photo-copies of it and pinned it up with a copy of the ad all over the Terrible House of Sickness. By the time Peter showed up on Saturday there wasn't one punk in Toronto who hadn't laughed his or her fuckin' head off at the photo. When Peter saw these photocopies pasted up on every wall, and everybody smirking at him, he turned fuckin' red. I had never seen anybody literally turn red before. He found an excuse to leave quickly, and nobody ever saw him again!

•••

The great thing about hanging around with Sickness was getting respect. All the clubs, Larry's Hideaway, The Turning Point, The Beverly Tavern or even The Horseshoe treated us like punk royalty. Punks begged us to come to their shows. You must have real punks like Sickness or the Morning Sickness Girls at your gig if you want your band to be taken seriously. We always got in free because we gave free beer to the bands if they came to the Terrible House afterwards. Just to make sure, we all wore big stickers on our leather jackets that said, 'I'm on the guest list, OR ELSE!' That was no joke; Ringo really did blow up and break heads sometimes.

I love punk rock because it's loud and fast and makes you slam. Guitars and bass thump like a fuckin' heart attack, and you can jump off the stage and nobody cares. The only other rule is that the band can't play covers. If you do, you get beer bottles thrown at your head. I don't know how anybody can listen to the homogenized shit on the radio. It's slow and overproduced, and the lyrics don't mean anything. And worst, you're a dumb schmuck who never meets the band and gets served ten millionth in line in this world of capitalist scum.

Toronto was the fuckin' greatest. It had so much awe-inspiring music that most of the time we never listened to bands from anywhere else. There was Sickness, of course, who urged punks to beat up business scum and break their cars. Then there was Direct Action who all had identical black hair that stuck up in every direction. They were the favourite band of slam dancers because they played harder and faster than anybody else. They all lifted weights and had huge chest and arm muscles bulging out of ripped black T-shirts. They had named themselves after a terrorist group in France, so the RCMP put them on a list of dangerous people and bugged their phones. Fuck, I made an alphabetical list of all the Toronto bands I saw with the Morning Sickness girls and put it in my diary. I still have it. Just reading the list sounds like poetry. There was A Neon Rome who faked a blood bath every show and who had bad hang-ups about going to Catholic school. Their most popular tune was *Jesus Motherfuck.* Then there was APB who were like a junior version of Direct Action. There were the Baby Slitters who were an all-girl band that Regan joined because we couldn't get Morning Sickness together. There was Baby Turns Blue, Berlin Wave, Blue Peter, The Bop Cats, Breeding Ground, Brontocrushrock and Bunchofuckingoofs, who were just like Sickness. I saw the Cardboard Brains and Chronic Submission who were all fourteen years old, but played thrash core so tightly and so fast that you'd think they had been rehearsing together for ten years. They all wore tight tie-dyed jeans and shaved their heads. It was too bad they turned into real skin-heads later. I liked them better when they got along with punks. I saw Crash Kills Five, The Dave Howard Singers, who were really just one maniac with an electric piano. I drank beer with Dick Duck and the Dorks whose singer ran off and married Nina Hagen. The rest of those guys became bouncers and never got a band together after that. I saw the Diodes who started Toronto punk, Direct Action, Disband, Dishes, Doomed Youth, and the Forgotten Rebels who were really from Hamilton, but played Toronto all the time. Every time the Rebels came to town, it was one big party at Larry's Hideaway. Everybody sang along with *Elvis is Dead, No Beatles Reunion,* and *Surfing on Heroin.* Then there was Groovy Religion, The Government, and The Jolly Tambourine Man, who were fuckin' fantastic. There was L'Etranger who dressed, danced and did harmonies like the Clash, but were really boring. There was Living Proof, Mike Marley and the Sailors who weren't reggae but sheer raunch, Negro Jazz Funeral, Norda, Northern Assault, Prisoners of Conscience, The Polka-holics, Primal Scream, Random Killing, Rim Code, Screaming Sam, Secrets, Stark Naked and the Fleshtones, Sudden Impact, Swindled, The Decapitated, The Gospel Shop, The Ministry of Love, who all lived in a house called The Church of the Fallen Elvis, United State, The Monsters, The Rent Boys Inc., The Ugly Models, Wild Things, The Young Lions, and Youth Youth Youth who weren't as good as people said they were. That's a fuck of a lot of bands for a sixteen-year-old girl to see, live, and party with. I even hung out with The Dub Rifles who came over from Winnipeg, and the guys from Victoria's Dayglo Abortions.

But not all those bands were fuckin' orthodox punk. Despite what rockers and music critics believe, punks are the most open-minded people when it comes to new types of music. They've heard of every fuckin' trend five years before anybody else. For example, there was a band called the Rent Boys, who faked British accents because 'rent boy' is British slang for male prostitute. They were real punks, but they played popping bass and talked about how 'funk' was the future. But if you ask me, funk is just another word for fuckin' disco. The Rent Boys were popular, but I never liked them. One time they bought plane tickets to London, England thinking they'd become famous. Their big triumph was when Melody Maker reviewed their show -- but just to laugh at them! The Brits must have thought those fake accents sounded pretty fuckin' stupid. Besides, bands that copied Heaven 17 had gone out of fashion a year before in England.

United State were a bunch of part-time punks who made the famous Toronto punk-umentary *Not Dead Yet,* and Groovy Religion, who I mentioned earlier, were a bunch of heroin addicts and played in slow motion.

There were also some very rotten bands. I don't mean rotten like the Rent Boys. At least they were trying. I mean people who should have just slit their wrists. For example, there was a band called Change of Heart who once opened for The Jolly Tambourine Man at The Beverly Tavern on Queen Street. Here was Jolly, with this fat singer named Steve in a rockabilly quiff and black leather jacket who did fearsome kung fu kicks to keep the slam dancers from climbing up to dive from the stage while he sang about running the Salvation Army down with a bakery truck. Everybody was slam dancing and laughing their heads off. And opening for them was Change of Heart, the lamest band I ever saw. They had this whining little twerp for a singer who plugged his guitar into a dozen effects pedals that mommy bought him so he could sound like The Cure. The Cure! Can you believe it? The Cure are the darling band of part-time punks everywhere. If you can't come up with your own sound or write songs about anything else but how depressed you are trying to get out bed in the morning, why bother? All the real punks went downstairs to drink until Change of Heart's set was over. Even the part-time punks left and asked for their money back 'cause they sensed something wasn't cool when the real punks left.

There's one more band I want to tell you about, but didn't before because they were even greater than Sickness, and I wanted to save them for last. A band so fuckin' nuts that even Steve and the other members of Sickness were afraid of them, the only band known to have put a live hamster in the blender on stage: the one, the only, the unforgettable Blibber and The Rat Crushers! They sang songs about going to Burger King and having your meal interrupted by retarded kids having sex. I knew it was true because I worked at Burger King, and I tell you it happened sometimes and weirder things too. The children's aid workers sometimes brought a group of ten or fifteen retards in. The mongo-loids kept talking about sex and made up stupid songs about anything that came into their heads. Sometimes when the aid workers turned their backs, some of those drooling idiots would get out of their leotards and trusses and fuck on the tables. The customers would try to ignore what was happening. I bet those people blocked it out of their memories and never mentioned it to their friends or families. Blibber and the Rat Crushers got up on stage and sang all about it. That's why they were true artists. They took the details of life that your average normalism forces himself to ignore and made art that forced everybody to notice. Blibber fans had T-shirts with a big 'B' in a circle that pissed off the purist anarchists because it was a parody of the 'A' in a circle. What made those anarchists turn purple with rage was when the fans jumped up and down and screamed, "Blibberchy, Blibberchy, Blibberchy." I still remember the lyrics to the final verse of *Stairway to Burger King,* a parody of Led Zeppelin's *Stairway to Heaven.*

As I walk into Burger King
I hear retarded children sing
How Lisa works at Burger King,
Eats up the burgers, spits out everything
I order food, it takes so long
I write down the retards' song
And as they begin to have sex
I feel my stomach begin to wretch
I sing their song for one and all
Two all beef patties on a roll
And she's buuuuying a Staaaaaaairway to
Burger King...

After every performance the crowd laughed and cheered and demanded an encore. And somebody always bought the band beers - two for every member - which wasn't really necessary because Blibber were always so drunk they were falling down and throwing each other out of the band on stage. That is, if they weren't too drunk to remember each other's names.

It's not true that Fresh Fish, Blibber's singer, put a live hamster in the blender at every show. That only happened once, and he didn't swallow the red furry goo like they said. He only gargled it and spat it out over the slam dancers. Unfortunately, he made a bunch of skinheads sticky, and that's why he got beat up. The story got around, and people started showing up at every Blibber and The Rat Crushers' gig expecting to see him do it again. It's amazing how stupid people -- even full-time punks -- can be.

Speaking of stupid people, the bad part about living on the scene was the glue-sniffing skinheads. A few months after I moved into the Terrible House of Sickness, dozens of skinheads started coming to shows to sniff airplane glue out of brown paper bags. Sickness hated that because glue makes people drool and it kills enough brain cells to make you permanently stupid. Skinheads are all stupid and have IQ's lower than dogs anyway, but it was sickening to see gangs of people with red noses and reeking of glue, kicking the shit out of innocent people. So if a skinhead sniffed glue from a brown paper bag at a show, Steve Sickness or Ringo snuck up with a lighter and exploded the glue head's lungs as he or she inhaled. Many skins were permanently cured of glue sniffing after their heads exploded. Sickness even wrote a song called *Exploding Glue Heads* that was a big sing-a-long hit and made everybody laugh. But it never got on the album, which was too bad, because I think it was their best number.

Things were bad enough when those fuckin' skinheads showed up, but things really started to fuck up one day when these seven bikers moved in. They were fat longhaired guys over thirty, and they were welcome because Assault, the main biker, was Ringo's brother. Punk rockers are supposed to hate bikers, and bikers are supposed to harass and beat up punk rockers, but they got along just fine. Now the beer drinking went on twenty-four hours a day, and more bikers visited. They didn't have any respect for women. As soon as a girl got near one these guys he'd pull her down onto his lap call her his 'pig'. They'd mix heavy metal records, shit like Metallica, with punk. It was so loud that I couldn't block it out by covering my ears. I couldn't sleep at all and I got fired from my job at Burger King 'cause I fell asleep on my shift.

By that time, I had 200 bucks saved up for an emergency. I kept it in the lining of my jacket. One afternoon I was alone at the house and Assault came in, beat me up, and took my money because he wanted it to buy beer and hash. I was afraid to tell Steve or Ringo about it because I didn't want to put a strain on our friendship. When rent time came, I told them I was broke. They were nice about it and told me I could have free beer and stay at the house for a few weeks until I got another job, but for food, I had to shoplift at supermarkets, and I was com-pletely miserable.

Then, to make everything really bad, Sickness got into a war with a skinhead gang 'cause they had lit the skinhead gang leader's glue bag and scorched his lungs. It wasn't safe to walk around Kensington Market or see bands unless escorted by Sickness or their biker pals.

These skinheads called their gang The Barf Puppies. They tried to make a band, but they were always too fucked up on glue to get any music together. Skinheads sometimes hang out with punks, but they're not punks. Violence doesn't just happen with them -- they go out looking for it. The Barf Puppies stopped punks in the street and robbed them of their leather jackets. They followed them home, trashed their houses and walked away with their record collections. Steve had to put a twenty-four hour guard and barbed wire around the house. He and Ringo vowed they'd drive The Barf Puppies out of Toronto. Sickness extended their protect-ion to any punk who had been wronged and started carrying around lists of names of skins who had to have their skulls crushed. They withdrew all protection from anybody who sniffed glue unless they signed a glue-aholics anonymous pledge.

The main skinhead was a tough guy named Fido. One time he walked into a party at some punk's house, ripped the door off the fridge, picked up somebody's cardboard six-pack of bottled beer and threw it down on the floor hard enough to smash the glass. Then he lifted it above his head and drank it. How can a person do that and not be dead from glass shards in his throat and stomach? That's how tough and stupid Fido was.

Anyway, Sickness and the bikers made a raid on Barf Puppy Palace and beat the hell out of them all. They had a list of all the stolen items and they put the leather jackets, boots, records and everything on the list in a van and took it away to the Terrible House of Sickness, where the real owners could pick it up. They gave those glue sniffing skinhead morons twenty-four hours to get out of town or die. The skin-heads packed off to Montreal and things got back to normal for a while.

I continued to live at the Terrible House of Sickness and shoplift my food and put up with the bikers. One day Dog shaved her head and had a fight with Bambi, so she switched sides and went to live with what was left of The Barf Puppies in Montreal. I began to think that the politics of the house were stupid, but there was no way I was going back to live with my mother and Brad. I didn't know what to do, and I was miserable.

One night around two A.M., everybody was partying at The Terrible House, and suddenly The Barf Puppies showed up in the street with thirty new skinheads nobody had ever seen before. Nobody even knew they were back in Toronto. We could hear Fido's voice screaming over a megaphone outside. It took me a moment to make out what he was saying. The idiot was taunting everyone and challenging Sickness to a fight. He was even trying to be a comedian and tell jokes! Can you believe it?

"How many fuckin' punk rockers does it take to screw in a fuckin' light bulb at a fuckin' Sickness show? Huh? I'll fuckin' tell you. One hundred! One to do the screwing in and ninety-nine on the fuckin' guest list! Har Har Har. Come out and get your fuckin' heads beat in or we'll come in and fuckin' beat them in for you!"

Then there was a lot of rushing around and people were out on the street and the house was full of Barf Puppies breaking everything with chains and bicycle parts. The stereo got smashed and Bambi's head got cracked. I ran out, pushing past Fido and some other skins, and got my arm torn with a knife. I ran a few blocks, heard police sirens, and ran to a park where I hid behind the trees. I stayed there for a few days, sleeping like the bums, and keeping one eye open so that none of the perverts that came there at night could come near me.

Chapter Three

After two or three days of living in the park behind trees, trying my best to stay away from perverts and police, I started to stink. The sweat from my armpits made the cotton of my T-shirt stick flat to my skin, and when I unzipped my leather jacket, a nasty smell wafted up. I felt like puking myself. I could feel my jeans cling to the insides of my legs as I walked. Fuck, I thought, my crotch must be fetid with sweat. I had never been so dirty, and I was getting zits all over. I couldn't see them, but I could feel them every-where as itchy bumps. There was no way I was going to get undressed to check my body, not even in the toilets in the park. Would a pervert even want me?

My green hair, which had looked so shocking and pretty after a bit of crimping and hair spray, was a stinking green rat's nest. I could hardly think because I felt so weak and hungry, but when I did, I got panicky because I remembered those Barf Puppy skinheads attacking the Terrible House of Sickness. Were Steve and Ringo dead? Were they in jail with the skinheads? Where the fuck could I wash safely? And what could I eat? I'd rather die than go back to my mother's in this state. There was no-where for me to live in this world, and that's all I ever wanted, somewhere to live in peace and the right to wear what I wanted to. I just cried. I didn't know what the fuck to do.

I looked around the park hoping that somebody I knew would come around, but nobody came. I stayed behind the trees and got dirtier and hungrier. By the third day I realized I had to eat and wash, scared or not. I couldn't just waste away and die. I left the park and started walking west along Dundas Street to the big Knob Hill supermarket at Lansdowne. A Trans Am slowed down and some rocker assholes screamed, "Fuck you, punk rock bitch!" I hardly noticed. All I knew was that Knob Hill was a big enough place that I could get lost in the crowds and pocket something. I had an urge to shoplift some burritos, and it was only a thirty-minute walk.

As I walked down the sidewalk, people started crossing the street when I got near them. It wasn't just that I was a tough looking punkette; it was because I smelled revolting. I liked people running away from me when I was a Morning Sickness Girl walking down the street with Melanie, Bambi and Dog, but now it was just freaky because this was the way it was whether I liked it or not. I got worried because my smell would attract too much attention for me to shoplift anything. I was never so fuckin' miserable in my life, but I kept walking anyway.

Then, just as I was coming up the hill outside the store, I saw Jane from Anarchy House who used to come to the parties at the Terrible House to distribute animal liberation pamphlets. I knew her even from behind because she was wearing that peasant dress with the big blue sunflower pattern and army boots. I was so fuckin' glad to see somebody, anybody, even stinky old Jane. She was the dirtiest person I knew. She didn't wash too often and had long, oily hair. I had really lucked out. She'd be the one least offended by my fuckin' horrible smell!

Even better than that, she was carrying a big bag of groceries. She was a vegetarian health freak. I knew she'd have that bag full with whole wheat bread and tofu dogs. It was so fuckin' good to see her.

I yelled out, "Hey Jane!" and ran up.

She yelled back, "Hey, Valerie Morning Sickness!"

This might be a good day after all.

I grabbed her hand and cried, "That asshole Fido and his Skinhead friends from Montreal attacked the Terrible House of Sickness! I ran away and I've been living in the park. I haven't talked to... I haven't seen anyone for three days. I don't know if Bambi or Melanie or anybody else is hurt or in jail or what! Those fuckin' skinheads broke everything. I ran out to the park because I was so scared, and I didn't even have time to get my stuff. I left all my records and clothes behind. And fuck, I fuckin' have no money! I've been living behind a bush in Trinity Bellwoods Park and nobody I knew came around. Do you know anything that's going on? Fuck, I stink! Sorry. I haven't eaten! Fuck, I need somewhere to wash, something, anything, to eat. Fuckin' help me, Jane, please!"

She gave me a hug and I cried more. I didn't mind that it was stinky Jane from Anarchy House who was always looking for any excuse to hug anybody. I didn't mind that I was talking to somebody over forty. She said, "OK. Let's go back to Anarchy House and we'll talk."

I followed her to the bus stop by the corner, and the bus came before anybody in the line up could get freaked out at my horrible fuckin' body stink.

We got on the bus and Jane paid our fare. The fat asshole of a bus driver looked at me for a moment as if he was going to throw me off, but then he clasped his nose and growled, "Get on!"

We went to the back and sat down. Jane knew I was fuckin' starved and said, "Why don't you have a look through the groceries and eat anything you want. It's OK. This is kind of an emergency for you."

So I went through the bag and ate an apple and two packages of uncooked tofu dogs and a half a loaf of whole wheat bread.

The only other person on the bus was an old lady, and she got off holding her nose at the next stop and shaking her head and muttering as if she wanted to murder us.

I ate and Jane told me about what hap-pened at The Terrible House of Sickness. "The story's been all over town, different versions. I heard that the police showed up about ten min-utes after the skins attacked. Do you remember any of that?"

"No", I said with half a tofu dog sticking out my mouth.

"Then you must have left at the beginning of it all. What I heard is that the police knew who lived at the house because they'd been around so often. They knew about how the skins had been robbing punks. They were pretty much on the side of Sickness, so they busted Fido and a bunch of the skins. The place is now in a shambles. Everything was broken, and even the door and the windows are gone. I have no idea where everybody is. Only Steve and Ringo live there now. They're trying to fix it back up. Sickness, Blibber and the Rat Crushers, Direct Action, and a bunch of other bands are putting together a benefit show at Larry's Hideaway next week so they can get money to start patching up the house."

I was so happy to be eating something, and so happy to hear that nobody was busted or dead. I just cried some more.

Jane said, "We'll be at Anarchy House in five minutes. You can get washed and sleep, and then we can talk more about it tomorrow."

I nodded.

We rode towards Bloor Street and I ate more tofu dogs. Finally we got to Anarchy House, which was just a normal looking family house in a long row of houses somewhere around Dufferin and Bloor. We climbed the steps to the front porch and Jane pushed the door open. "It's never locked," she said.

A bunch of old punks were there, three or four guys in their twenties. They were lying on the sofa or floor in the living room like slobs. They looked up as we came in the door, but they were busy watching something on video and didn't say hello. Then I recognized the one lying in front of the TV. His name was George, and he had moved out of the Terrible House about the time I moved in. He used to sing for Prisoners of Conscious before they broke up.

I said, "Hi George!" But he was too list-less to answer. What was with his clothes? He used to wear ripped jeans and an

Exploited T-shirt with a profile of Wattie with that huge spiked mohawk gobbing on the crowd. Now he was wearing a pink pastel tie-dyed sweatshirt and baggy jeans like a hippy. Fuck, he sure had gotten pale and skinny since last time I saw him. I wondered what had happened, but didn't have the energy to ask. Well, there would be time tomorrow.

Jane took me to the bathroom upstairs and left me there to shower. It was a dirty bathtub, but no worse than the one at the Terrible House of Sickness. There was an old cracked bar of soap in the bottom. I turned the taps and made enough lather from the soap to wash my hair. Old hair spray makes the water black when you rinse it out. You usually have to wash and rinse two or three times, but my hair was so fuckin' filthy with old hair spray and dirt from the park that the water was black up to the tenth rinse. I watched the filthy water swirl down the drain.

Finally, I dried myself and left the bath-room wearing a towel because my clothes were too dirty to wear.

Jane was waiting by the door with one of her peasant dresses hanging over her arm. She said, "Here, you can sleep in this." Then she took me down the hall and pointed me to the back bedroom. I went in and looked around. There was a window and a wicker chair. Jane had put my stinking clothes in a plastic bag in the corner. She pointed to them and said, "You can get those washed later. We'll talk after you get some sleep." Then she said good night, even though it was only about two o'clock in the afternoon, and closed the door.

I yanked the peasant dress off and threw it on a chair because I hated it. Wearing it even for a few minutes made me feel baggy assed. Then I lay down and passed out on the futon.

I opened my eyes and saw that I was in a strange bedroom with a chair made of straw in the corner. I was lying on a futon and the morning sun was coming in a window above my head somewhere.

For a second I wondered where the fuck I was, thinking this was some kind of dream. Then I remembered meeting Jane. I remembered that she took me back to Anarchy House, her house, and that's where I was now.

OK, at least I wasn't rotting away and smelling like shit behind a bush in a park any-more. I suddenly got paranoid. Was Jane going to let me stay here more than one night? We weren't exactly close. We didn't talk about that yesterday. I didn't know how to ask her.

I put on the peasant dress and looked in the mirror. It looked stupid on me. I walked downstairs to the kitchen. Nobody was up. The clock said it was five-thirty in the morning. The white walls of the kitchen glowed a pinkish colour in the morning sun. It was pretty. I had never got up to appreciate the colour of the morning sun before in my life. I was still nervous.

There was some Nescafé in the cupboard and I made coffee because it seemed like an adult thing to do. I wondered what Jane was doing with coffee in her house. I thought an anarchist vegetarian freak like her would only have herbal tea. I found some milk in the fridge. If I was going to stay at a vegetarian anarchist's house, at least she wasn't a fuckin' vegan. Vegans are the preachiest type of fuckin' vege-tarians.

I watched the clock for twenty minutes waiting for somebody to get up. Nobody did. I went back to bed but didn't sleep. I was so anxious that I lay there trying to find patterns in the stucco of the ceiling. A couple of blue jays fluttered and chirped outside then left. It was hell being too anxious to sleep but bored enough to want to sleep.

Finally, I heard some noises in the kitchen. I got up again and went downstairs. It was Jane spreading some green vegetable goo on whole-wheat toast. She was naked, and her fat tits were saggy, nipples pointing to the floor.

She said, "Good morning Valerie."

I said, "Good morning," and tried not to look shocked. I was thinking that if I said the wrong thing she might tell me that I had to leave the house by the end of the day. I said, "I drank some coffee, I hope that's OK."

"Great, make me a cup. I can't wake up without it, you know how it is."

I made two cups. Then I regretted making myself one because it might seem as if I was taking too many liberties. I was getting more paranoid when what I really wanted was to be calm enough to ask important questions. I said, "Milk?"

"Sure."

Then we drank coffee together for a few moments and Jane pushed her long greasy black hair out of her eyes. She said, "I can't get going without my coffee in the morning because me and the boys were doing ecstasy again last night."

I said, "What do you mean, 'again?' Do you do that often?"

She said, "Yeah, three or four times a week. Whenever we feel like it."

I changed the subject. "I just want to thank you for saving me from that park yester-day."

"You're welcome," she said sipping. "It's Monday morning, Valerie. Weekend's finished. I have to get to work."

I didn't know anarchists worked. I didn't know what to say. Then I tried to make some small talk. I said, "Where do you work?"

She said, "Out in the suburbs, Missis-sauga, in my uncle's office. This is his house. He lets me keep it as I want. He doesn't care."

Then she sat up, looked at me straight, and said what I wanted to hear, "Do you want to live here?"

"Yes."

"Then here's the deal. You can have the back bedroom for a hundred and fifty bucks a month. If you have no money I can waive the rent for the first two months and lend you another hundred so that you can get a few cheap clothes and look for a job."

I said, "Thank you, Jane." It sounded like a great deal.

"Not so fast. Listen, Valerie, I live an alternative lifestyle. Can you understand that? Me and the guys who live here, George, Tyler, Pete and Bob are lovers. That's the alternative lifestyle here at Anarchy House. I know you need a place. You can stay here. You can live your life how you want to live it, but

I don't need any prudes or anybody insulting us behind our backs for the way we live. Do you understand that?"

I said, "OK. I can understand that. Hey, I'm not prejudiced."

I hoped that she would believe me. I'm not prejudiced. I didn't care how Jane lived. It was her business. I didn't care that she was over forty and looked really dumpy and out of shape. It's just that it was all a little new and shocking. I never even imagined a woman who kept four lovers in a house.

Jane said, "Good. You can hang around the house or do what you like. Food is in the fridge. Help yourself. I have to get to work now. Oh yeah, there's one more rule. You can eat eggs or cheese, but this is a vegetarian house. Meat is murder. Remember that!"

Then she dragged her saggy tits off to the bedroom again while I sipped on my coffee. She came out with that same old peasant dress with the faded blue sunflowers. Her hair was all over her shoulders. She explained, "Uncle Joseph doesn't care how I dress. Seeya later." Then she left.

Relieved, I went back to bed and slept. When I got up again, it must have been almost eleven. I put my own peasant dress on and went downstairs to see if anyone else was around.

George and Tyler were there. George had changed and was wearing his black leather jacket and green combat pants. Tyler was more of a hippy. He was wearing tie-dyes and had hair halfway down his back.

I said, "Hi."

Tyler said, "Yeah, we remember you, Valerie. From the night we had a party and the Morning Sickness Girls came over."

I said, "Really!" It was a compliment that he remembered me.

George said, "Yeah, you drank so much you puked in the bathtub."

I said, "Shit, I don't remember that! Fuck! I'm really sorry."

"Don't sweat it, man. It happens to us all. I hear you're staying here now."

I said, "Yeah."

Tyler said, "Listen, it's eleven o' clock, and we've got some friends coming over for a committee meeting. You can stay and listen if you like, but none of your comments will be official because you don't have a place on the committee, and you will just be part of the gallery."

I wasn't sure what he was talking about, but I wanted to get along with everybody, so I said, "OK."

Then we sat around the living room and George rolled a joint while we watched a video about how lab animals are tortured and how we could organize raids on labs to liberate them. Then Pete and Bob came into the living room and Pete, who was wearing a black leather jacket like a punk but was going bald said, "Hello," and puffed on the joint and sat back in the chair. And Bob, who was just a guy in a T-shirt and underwear, said he was having a paranoia attack from coming down off ecstasy and had to go back to the bedroom to sleep.

Then a bunch of weird longhairs, hippies, four or five of them, came over. George turned the video off and we sat around the sofa and floor and had a meeting. The meeting was mostly George talking. He went on about how meat is murder and animals are equal to humans, and how we should all liberate lab animals. You know, the usual anarchist stuff. Sometimes one of the hippies asked him to repeat something so he could write it down on a blue notepad.

Well, that got really boring after about five minutes, so I went back to my bedroom where I slept for maybe an hour. Then I woke up but just lay around bored on the bed. I went back downstairs and George was still going on about some plan to instil social anarchy in high schools by setting up a worldwide system of after-school anarchist clubs. I hated listening to him, so I went outside and sat on the front balcony and watched the old Italian guy next door water his concrete path with a green hose. That got boring too, so I went back inside and George and his hippy friends were still talking about anarchy. In the kitchen, I made myself a tofu dog sandwich with mayonnaise and lots of relish and went back to the bedroom to eat it. After that, I came downstairs and made some coffee, and I could still hear George talking about anarchy. I thought he'd never fuckin' shut up. I spent the rest of the afternoon in my bedroom with my pillow over my head, trying to rest.

Around five o'clock, I heard the anarchy meeting breaking up, with those weird hippies saying goodbye at the door. Down in the living room, George was watching another video about how animals are tortured to test cos-metics. Then Tyler rolled a joint and we smoked it. Even Bob, the paranoid guy, came out of the bedroom to take a puff and we all waited for Jane to get back.

I said, "Do you have meetings often?"

But George gave me this serious look and pointed at a monkey on the video with its head in a vice being made to smoke itself to death and said, "Just look at this, man. It's really heavy. Look at what they're doing to that monkey."

We watched the depressing video and got more stoned. Finally, Jane got home and made dinner for everybody, some green vegetable goo spread on whole-wheat bread with herb tea. Then we smoked a joint and listened to punk rock, the Young Lions tape. After that, Jane and her boyfriends did ecstasy and disappeared into the bedroom, leaving me alone to listen to music or watch TV and get bored. Anarchy House lacked the excitement of the Terrible House of Sickness. I didn't even want to think about how they had sex. Did they poke themselves into her loose and out of shape ass and mouth and cunt all at once, or did they line up?

Next day I woke up, put on the peasant dress and bought some brown hair dye to get my hair back to its normal colour. By about twelve I looked OK, and by one o'clock I was in Kensington Market buying a couple of used blouses and skirts. I passed by the broken glass at the Terrible House, but didn't go in to check if Steve and Ringo were there. I wanted to put that part of my life behind me. I spent the rest of the afternoon downtown asking restaurants if they needed a waitress. When I got back to Anarchy House at five-thirty, the hippy guys were just leaving. They had just finished another meeting.

At six, Jane came home and we had dinner -- yellow and red vegetable goo on whole wheat bread. We smoked a joint and listened to punk music before she and her boyfriends dropped ecstasy and went into the back room again to fuck. I watched TV and listened to the Crass and Youth Youth Youth for a while. Then I got bored and went upstairs to my bedroom. I figured out that Anarchy House had the same fuckin' routine every fuckin' day, and I started hating my life there.

After about six weeks of pounding the streets, I got a job working as a waitress at the Golden Griddle on Carlton Street, the afternoon shift. That meant I was in the house all morning getting bored out of my mind by those videos of monkeys getting tortured to death and those anarchist meetings that started at exactly eleven A.M. Sometimes I was happy to go to work, even if I was just taking all-day breakfast orders from stupid fat business people. I started doing things in my time off that I'd never done before, like cleaning up the bathroom or mowing the lawn.

One morning when I was so bored with George that I felt like screaming, I went into Jane's room and started to look through the books on the shelf by her bed. There was the usual material you find at punk rockers' houses like the Anarchist's Cook Book, The Letters of Bakunin, and fanzines like Maximum Rock 'n' Roll. I looked through the stuff, but it was all so boring.

On the top shelf there was a novel called *The Little Fadette*. It was written a hundred years ago and translated from French. The back cover said that it was about a teenage girl going through some tough times as she grew up, and I thought that sounded like me. The author had a man's name, George Sand, even though she was a woman. I thought it was weird that a woman was named George, and that got me wondering what kind of book she wrote. I asked a French Canadian anarchist named Gilles, who was one of the hippies who came to George's meetings, if it was normal for French people to call women 'George'. He told me not to be stupid. I showed him the book, and he shrugged and said that maybe in France they did things differently than we do in Canada, French Canada, but that he had never met a woman named George.

The book was about an ugly girl growing up on the edge of a town where they raise fuckin' cows or something. Her mother is like a new age herbalist, but everyone calls her Bloody - Witch-Who-Ran-Off-With-A-Soldier. When the people get sick and the doctor can't help, all the respectable types end up searching out her mom in the forest and begging for herbal cures. Anyway, Fadette is the girl's nickname. It means Little Fairy Girl or something like that. But the other kids just call her 'Gremlin' and throw rocks at her head. When the rocks connect with her skull and she's fuckin' reeling in pain, they scream things at her like, "There goes the little screaming Gremlin. Hey, where is your deserter of a father? You don't know, and you're mother didn't follow him far enough if you're still in our town!" Then Fadette turns around and says something like, "By the love of the Holy Virgin I will never be ashamed of my dear sweet mama who bore me and my little brother André! And we will see who is judged righteous on the day of our Lord!" Then the other kids laugh and hit her head with more rocks.

I figured France must be a harsh place. Anyway, in the book, the local teenage stud is named Landry and he has a brother who is retarded and gets lost in a thunderstorm, and Landry thinks he's going to die if he doesn't find him. Fadette says she'll do some woodlands magic and make him turn up, but she sets one condition: Landry has to promise to dance with her in the town square on Sunday after church. He agrees, and she rescues the retard brother just before the river rises and sweeps him away. Sunday comes and Landry dances with her. The problem is that Landry has this snotty bitch named Madeleine for a girlfriend who goes on a vengeance trip. She throws more rocks at Fadette's head. Then Fadette goes through puberty and her tits grow out and she's no longer ugly, but beautiful, just like in the Ugly Duckling story. Landry falls in love with her, of course.

I don't know how it ends because it I stopped reading it. Fadette probably marries Landry while everyone throws rocks at bitch Madeleine's head.

I read the introduction just because I was bored, but the woman who translated it was really down on George Sand, and she wrote something like, "Characters with the same angst and anxieties as the all-too-neurotic authors are all too common, and *The Little Fadette* is no exception." I thought that was so fuckin' mean. What is a woman living in France a hundred years ago supposed to write about but the problems of French women living in France a hundred years ago? Is she supposed to write a book about a man living in China in the year 2150 who is an astronaut, has one leg and has his whole body tattooed purple? That's the fuckin' stupidest thing I ever heard! If I ever write a book, it will be about a girl putting up with the shit I had to put up with! You know, eating the fuckin' cabbage at my mother's and getting chased out of my living space by a bunch of asshole skinheads named The Barf Puppies.

I asked Jane what she thought about the book, and she shrugged her shoulders. She said her brother had given it to her, and that she hadn't got round to reading it yet. That's how bored I got at fuckin' Anarchy House. I, Valerie Morning Sickness, the despair of English teachers, was actually reading.

And so life went on and three or four months passed and I got used to George making long speeches and I even began to sit in on the first hour of the eleven o'clock meetings before I worked my ass off at the Golden Griddle. I didn't know how George got the energy to talk because Jane didn't feed him much, and he was getting skinnier all the time. He preached on his version of social utopia: one day the establish-ment would disappear and countries would melt away. There would be no taxes, no police, and no money. People would live in collectives and do nothing but what they felt like. Marriage would disappear and sex would be spon-taneous. People would be fed with produce grown by the collectives, and everybody would be free to come and go as they pleased. All we had to do to realize this anarchist utopia was live the life we led at Anarchy House, and refuse to be used by the system of industrial fascist oppression around us. Besides that, we all had to be vegetarians, preach the message and parti-cipate in subversive activity. It was particularly important to destroy the banking system.

After listening to the things that George said about anarchy every day, I slowly got interested because I was so fuckin' bored. I needed something to do. Soon we were going on night raids at McDonald's to put crazy glue in the locks. Once we even broke into a research lab and freed a bunch of dogs that they were using to test hair spray. Before I knew it, I was becoming a real committed anarchist. We read pamphlets from California that told us how to cause lots of damage. I still got one here above the fridge. It's so fuckin' over the top it's funny.

FUN WITH A GREASE BUCKET

This trick takes no brains or imagination, so that even you can strike back at the rotten social fabric. Behind McDonald's, usually next to the trashcans, there is a big barrel with the words, 'not fit for human consumption' or 'inedible contents'. They must have made a mistake. These labels belong on the food, not the grease barrel. The lid is on tight for a reason. It smells as if somebody died from the rancid Chicken McNuggets and they put the body in the barrel to let it rot for a couple of months. It's easy to open. Undo the ring around the top and open the lid. Don't forget to wear a damp handkerchief over your face as you do this. The pong will cover the entire parking lot in about two minutes. Customers will throw up and leave. You can tip the barrel on a warm day. The sun will do the rest.

Pretty wild, eh? And to think I actually used to do such things!

One Saturday night we were having a party and the discussion got heated. Jane was handing out the McDonald's pamphlet to every-body. She wanted to get a spontaneous raid happening and get some new people involved. This one guy who had a bit of alcohol in him turned to her and said that social disruptions like that were too weak to change society because the restaurant owners would just think they were vandalized by some frustrated neighbourhood kids showing off to each other, and the animal testers would just get new animals. The Anarchist message was pointless because it always got lost.

And Jane got indignant and answered, "Who thinks that? Only you and a few establishment pigs, nobody else in this room!"

But the guy wasn't about to be made to look stupid and said, "Nah, I used to be an anarchist, but now I read Aleister Crowley. Do what thou wilt shall be the whole of the Law. Crowley says that the anarchists who set off the bomb in the Hay Market in Chicago a hundred years ago did nothing but give the authorities an excuse to hire more police. Most anarchists grow out of vandalizing stuff and learn to see things that way."

Jane went into a rage and started screaming that that was bullshit because Aleister Crowley was Satan. You would have thought she was a rabid born-again Christian rather than an anarchist. Then she went into some rhetoric about how great blazes started from little sparks, and waved some pamphlets in the guy's face. The guy laughed and said that he had no fear of unrestrained anarchists, seeing what a feeble bunch of clowns everybody at the house was. He said that if repressed neurotics such as the police were ever left unrestrained by their social conditioning they might turn into a bunch of ferocious animals and do us all in, and if any-thing, society, repressive as it was, kept people as bad as the police locked in their roles so that the rest of us were more or less safe.

Then Jane started yelling and repeating herself and swinging the table lamp around by the cord as if she was going to bust the guy's head open. But he laughed at her with this laugh as if he was Satan himself, and she had to calm down by taking a couple of ecstasy pills and going away to have sex with Tyler and Bob. Jane cancelled the raid, and a story passed around the punk rock community about what a lame bunch of pseudo-anarchists lived at 'Anarchy House.'

I didn't listen to what the guy who read Crowley said; I was still as enthusiastic an anarchist as ever, but he really squelched Jane's enthusiasm for the cause, and from that night things started to go lame. Every time we planned a raid on a McDonald's or a Burger King it got cancelled because Jane suddenly decided to drop a couple hits of ecstasy and have sex with George and Tyler and Bob and Pete. One night I went through a lot of trouble to change shifts at the Golden Griddle just to be part of a raid, and she cancelled at the last minute because everybody did ecstasy. I was really pissed off.

I finally lost faith in the members of the house as anarchists after the Anarchist Picnic in Buffalo, New York State. That's when I realized that Jane and her skinny boyfriends had no commitments except to their freaky sex lives, and that if anybody was going to be a committed anarchist, it was going to be me. We all went down to Buffalo by bus, but just before we got to the US border, all the Anarchy House denizens but me dropped some 'E' (That's slang for ecstasy). I bleached my hair and spiked it up for the occasion, and even the anarchy house members travelled in their torn leather jackets. Jane just wore that ugly peasant dress and her army boots. When we got to Customs, the guard looked at Bob real mean and said, "You're coming inside to talk to me because you look anti-social." That was too bad because Bob was the one who got paranoid easily. That happened just as the ecstasy was coming on and Bob got into some nervous sweats. The guards questioned him for a good half-hour and it held the bus up. The other passengers looked at us as if they wished the American border cops would take us all out, put us against a brick wall and shoot us. Bob thought he was going to have a heart attack. They took him to a concrete room without windows and rubber gloved him 'cause they wanted to see if he was carrying any drugs up his butt. People say that nobody can have a bad experience on E, but pain is still pain. Sometimes it's more intense, like for example when some snarling American border cop puts his hand up your ass. Bob, with intensified physical sensations from the drug, probably felt the same with the finger stuck up his ass as he would if the guard had stuck a fire hydrant up there. He fuckin' screamed, but that just made the border guards laugh. Jane didn't get rubber gloved, but that was only because she stinks.

Anyway, they let us pass in spite of the fact that Jane and her boyfriends were glassy-eyed, and soon we were at the Buffalo bus station where some anarchists were already hanging around.

There was a mini-bus full of anarchist kids from Ottawa with hair down past their asses. They were collecting a few friends from the buses coming from various cities to take them out to the site of the Anarchist Picnic, which was a few miles away in a park on the east side of the city. An Ottawa anarchist in a T-shirt with a huge 'A' in a circle on front and back came to me and said he thought I was cool because I was wearing my black leather jacket despite there being so many militant vegans around. We got to talking and he said his mini-bus had an extra seat. I got in, and Jane said that she and the other four would try to hitch a ride.

This is where the story gets strange, but it's true. Jane, George, Pete, Tyler and Bob got a ride almost right away. I know, 'cause I saw them getting into the car as the mini-bus pulled out. Now that sounds almost impossible, because nobody in their right mind would stop to pick up a gang of glassy-eyed leather jacketed punks with a baggy middle-aged woman in a peasant dress who stank. But if you've ever dropped E, you know that magical friendly things just happen to you. Well, some guy with a moustache who looks like an off-duty cop pulls over and offers them a ride in his car and he says he'll take them to the picnic site. All five of them hop into the back seat, Jane and her four scrawny geek boyfriends. The guy who is doing the driving keeps turning his head backwards to talk to them as he's driving, so he's not really watching the road. They can see from his eyes, which are bugging out, that he's on ecstasy too, which seems natural to them. Now, like I said, it may seem strange that five people hitchhiking on ecstasy get picked up right away by a guy who himself is blitzed on the same drug. But these magical things just seem to happen on E. There's no explaining it.

Anyways, the guy keeps turning his head around to talk. But they're all feeling so good about everything that they don't care. They're just rubbing themselves up against the car seats so they can feel the beauty of the texture of the leather. The guy tells them that his name's Michael and he has a lot more E. He opens his glove compartment, throws a plastic bag of pills into the back, and tells them to take as many as they want. It was all so friendly that they pass the bag around and they all swallow four or five pills each. The E is so strong that the effects start to set in after a few minutes and that makes them all feel horny. Jane noticed that they were going the opposite direction from the park, but she didn't care about anything except doing something about her horniness.

They don't even know what this stranger who fed them full of E plans to do with them, or why he is driving away from the picnic site, or where they are really going. They are just so horny they are going insane and George rips off Jane's underwear and the four of them turn her upside down and start to munch down on her. They rip all their clothes off and start having an orgy in the back seat of the car. And the guy at the wheel is driving with his head backward and he's getting really excited and encourages them. All the time he's yelling out, "Yeah! Yeah! Go for it! Yeah!" Over and over again.

Suddenly the guy runs a red light and smashes into a car. This accident happens in the Portuguese part of Buffalo where people are really tough. Anyway, these four Portuguese guys get out of the car that's been hit and when they see that they had their car smashed by a bunch of naked maniacs, they're mad as hell. They are not compassionate and they pull the guy out of the front seat of the car and start beating his head in with a set of golf clubs they took from their trunk. Jane and her minions somehow escape by running off in different directions, but they're naked and hallucinating and in a strange part of town in a foreign country. They lose each other, and it's getting dark by this time, so they hide naked in alleys and doorways. They pass the night shivering and stealing clothes from laundromats and washing lines and pawing themselves at every opportunity because they are so horny they can't help but masturbate.

The next day they all managed to gather where the picnic had been even though they missed it. They didn't have any money or pass-ports and they were starved and paranoid, but Jane somehow got in touch with some anarchist friends who put all four of them in the trunk of a car and took them back across the border to Canada.

At least I got to enjoy the picnic. There were some speeches, black anarchist flags, a lot of American anarchists and punks. There was even a performance by a Detroit punk band called Son of Sam, which impressed me because it seemed less incestuous than Toronto Punk. The band didn't seem to care if anybody knew who they were or not. They just played straight-forward hardcore, rubbed beer and sweat into their spiky black hair, and spat out large mouth-fuls of beer and water on the slam dancing crowd as they sang about civilization coming to an end, starting with the car factories in Detroit.

When Jane and her boyfriends got back to Anarchy House, they talked for weeks about the fuck-up they had made of their stay in Buffalo as if their stupid misadventure had been some sort of achievement. I guess with every-body at Anarchy House being such losers I don't really have an excuse for living there a whole year. All I can say is that a private room in a real house is probably the best deal a sixteen-year-old girl can get for a hundred and fifty bucks a month.

But we weren't the only anarchist com-mune in the Toronto area. There were hundreds of people attempting anarchist lifestyles of one sort or another. There were a couple of guys in their forties who dressed like members of a nineteenth-century barbershop quartet. They had straw hats and drove around everywhere on a tandem bicycle. These weren't punk rock slobs. They were meticulously clean and spent their days distributing anarchist literature. The police never bothered them because they seemed like polite, clean-cut eccentrics. They named themselves Thing One and Thing Two, like in Dr Seuss' Cat in the Hat. I hung out at their house in Rosedale on Sundays and we watched Laurel and Hardy movies. There was a group of women called Fetal Stew who saw anarchy as the final expression of radical feminism. They were unattractive, overweight, dressed in flannel, and had formerly been Marxists. They resented men and saw them as animals. According to the literature they distri-buted, the imperialist male slave had its only function at this stage of evolution providing income for the female anarchist vanguard. To this end, they worked as prostitutes and distributed pamphlets encouraging all women to have the courage to do the same. I still have a copy of the pamphlet somewhere. It's called 'The Anarchist Sex Trade Worker', and starts with the slogan *'The sex trade is the only moral form of labour, for the worker controls entirely the means of production'.* These same women even released their own afterbirth/placenta cook-book. But I stopped hanging out at their house after they got pissed off with me because I refused to eat mother-earth-afterbirth-brownies. There were lots of other people too who had their own vision of how world anarchy could be realized, and each group was living radical lifestyles to set an example. Most considered Jane, and Anarchy House, to be a lame joke, and I was ashamed to live there.

Well, the guys I was telling you about in the straw hats that rode the tandem everywhere started planning a North American Anarchist Picnic. They decided to model it on the Buffalo picnic. They got permission from the City of Toronto to use a corner of Trinity Bellwoods Park and invited anarchist groups from all over the continent to attend. I spent a whole month of free time on Saturdays standing on the corner of Yonge and Queen handing out pamphlets.

Finally, the day came and there were anarchists from all over who had set up their little booths in the park. At one corner, over-looking it all, there was a four-foot stage with microphones and a speaker system big enough for an arena rock dinosaur band like Van Halen. Above the stage hung a long row of thirty black anarchist flags standing out against the blue sky as they blew in the wind, and even a few red and black flags. The red and black is a variation, but it is still the anarchist flag. The whole set-up made the people making speeches seem some-how dignified and important. Some of the purists didn't like it, and called it an anarchist Nuremberg, 'cause Hitler had used a stage like that.

I had come down in the morning with Jane. I took an ecstasy pill and was feeling happy to touch everything and even quite proud that I had had a hand in the preparations. The park was like a circus freak show. There was a booth of the ugliest women you ever saw. They were from Florida and all had breasts so large they almost toppled over. They were first at the mike, and they made a long speech about how women with painful, oversized breasts were the victims of the worst discrimination in society, and how anarchy presented the only solution. They also believed that men and women were separate species, even in the animal world, and that the sexes should live segregated as a first step before all men were cut up and destroyed as an inferior species. This was the next stage of evolution and would be realized within the next ten years when cloning became possible. When they got off the stage, they got into a screaming match with Fetal Stew, the Anarchist Sex Trade Workers, who insisted that anarchy could only be achieved if the male parasite was exploited as a source of income. The scuffle would have come to blows if Steve and Ringo from Sickness, who were acting as security, hadn't broken it up. The real police, the Toronto City Police, were hanging out on horses and waving night-sticks at the edge of the park. Next, some political science professor from the University of Toronto got up and gave a long boring lecture about Bakunin and the history of the anarchist movement and how the black flag worked against the aims of the anarchists because it was a sign of institutionalization. Nobody cared to listen.

An old woman named Ann got up on the stage next, and said that she had voted for the Progressive Conservative Party all her life until one day she was evicted from her house at sixty years old. She had then taught herself to play guitar and went everywhere singing a song called Right is Wrong. Next, a group of bald, overweight, middle-aged, homosexual punk rockers from Texas got up and apologized for being Communists. They said they had just come along to offer sympathy for the cause. Actually, these bald guys were the famous Texas punk band The Revolting Cocks, and they were really sneaking in some advertising for their show later that night at the Silver Dollar Club. They were double-billed with the Mentors. There were a hundred kids from Kansas who all walked around with the anarchist 'A' in a circle in white paint on the back of their black leather jackets. I tried to talk to some of them because they were about my age, but they had nothing to say, and never got up on stage. There were old hippies who smoked marijuana in defiance of the police. There were many tables with pamphlets, and even a few people plugging their own books. Besides the clash between the women with the huge breasts and the Sex Trade Workers, it was all quite peaceful and I talked to many people as I walked around the park. I was very happy and hugged everybody because I was so stoned.

It was such a beautiful sunny day, with a light breeze to make you perfectly comfortable. The whole punk rock scene came out, and there wasn't a skinhead in sight. I met people I hadn't spoken to since my days at the Terrible House of Sickness. I got news that Dog had died of a heroin overdose in Montreal and that Ringo's brother's bike gang had left town. Dog's death made me feel sad. I mean, Dog had been a Morning Sickness Girl, one of my gang, even if she had turned traitor and become a fuckin' skinhead Barf Puppy. I used to think she was immortal because I saw her win a PCP breath-holding contest in the bottom of a swimming pool.

I finally walked back through the trees to see what was happening on stage. Jane, George, and Tyler were sitting on the grass up front watching three scrawny men with ballerina skirts and beards squeal like castratos into the microphone. They had straggly hair down to their shoulders and I knew they must have been on speed because I could smell their sickly sweat from ten metres away. Jane pulled close to my ear and whispered that she had invited them to stay at Anarchy House until they went back to Vancouver in a few days. The scrawny men screamed gibberish into the microphone. I couldn't make sense of it at all, except that they felt they had realized their aims, whatever these aims were, by having sex with each other. They wore skirts to prove their 'omni-sexuality'. Then they invited everyone to come have sex with them at Anarchy House after the picnic. I squealed. I didn't want these weird freaks screwing at my house!

Jane grabbed my shoulder and said, "Don't worry, it will be all right". Then they gave our address and I started to shiver because I had a feeling that something terrible was going to happen. Then the men in skirts started screaming, "We are the Clouds! We are the Clouds! We are the Clouds!" into the microphone and that went on for fifteen minutes and I started laughing like I was mad because they were so absurd. Then one of the guys in a straw hat who rode the tandem, Thing Two, got up on stage and announced that the picnic was over and that there would be a demonstration in Queen's Park in front of the Ontario Legislature. Every group was to collect their black flag and display it proudly, so that the throng of anar-chists would appear like a parade.

I didn't want to see the horrible men in skirts have sex at my house, so I decided to follow the demonstration. I was a little ashamed that Anarchy House never got it together enough to make a black flag of its own. It was about a twenty-minute walk to Queen's Park, and the police on horses followed us all the way. People whispered to each other that whenever anybody held up a black flag and lit it on fire we were to swarm around it, and when they dropped the flag, held up a rattle, and blew a whistle, we were to run in all directions. I didn't understand.

When we got there, we stood around waiting for the others to arrive. Jane and my other housemates were nowhere around. I was happier to be in the park with all the anarchists than at the house with the Clouds performing weird sex acts in the living room.

After a while, all the anarchists had shuffled into the park. Someone started chanting "Anarchy! Anarchy! Anarchy!" at the top of her lungs, then everybody joined in, waving their fists in the air and chanting, "Anarchy! Anarchy! Anarchy!" Suddenly a black flag went up and burst into flames. I remembered what they said about the whistles and rattles, and ran over to the burning flag with everyone else. We all chanted, "Anarchy! Anarchy! Anarchy!" with our fists in the air. The police didn't like this, and rushed in on the horses with swinging batons. I was scared. I didn't want my head bashed in. Suddenly the woman holding the flag dropped it and another person blew a whistle and started swinging a football rattle like the ones the British use at soccer games. It made a terrible racket. That was the signal, and every-body suddenly ran in separate directions.

You should have seen the look on those stupid cops' faces! They didn't have a crowd to aim batons at, no target, only complete chaos. A horse whinnied in fright and another black flag went up in flame at the end of the park next to the statue of King Edward VII, Emperor of India, sitting on his horse. We rushed at it and started chanting, "Anarchy! Anarchy! Anarchy!" Again, the police reorganized their horses and rushed us, but just as they got close, the person holding the burning flag dropped it, blew a whistle and started waving another one of those noisy rattles. We ran in all directions. This was fun! Another flag went up in another corner of the park, this time a black and red one. It too burst into flame and those who were near rushed it and started chanting. The police had no contingency for this, so they rushed again, but the person dropped the flag, blew a whistle, waved a rattle and everybody dispersed. Another flag went up in flames, it was Regan from The Terrible House who waved it, and the police regrouped. It was magnificent! Here at the seat of Ontario government, anarchy and anarchists ruled. There was nothing the police or anybody else could do about it!

In the middle of the craziness, one of the men in straw hats, Thing One, took my arm and explained that this was a model for an anarchist society. If we could all be orderly in disorder like this all the time, then authority would be frustrated and disappear, leaving anarchist utopias as the social order for all time. Another flag went up in flames and we rushed at it together, chanting and waving our fists in the air. It was all so glorious, so wonderful to be a part of, and it seemed so *right*. Organized chaos had beaten authority if only for that afternoon. By the time a dozen or so flags had gone up in flame, dozens of police cars had arrived with sirens blaring. A dozen rattles crackled in the air and the men in straw hats bellowed through a megaphone that this was the final dispersal, and we all ran out into the streets in every direction. The police were able to arrest nobody, and nobody was hurt except for a few bruises from the batons.

A few blocks away, I met up with a couple of punks, Regan and Jennifer Ogilvie. I told Regan how proud I was of her, and she sucked up the praise with a big smile and scratched me affectionately with her two-inch nails. We decided to go to

Anarchy House to see what the Clouds were up to, and to see how many people were taking them up on their offer. We laughed madly all the way about how we had made fools of the police and the govern-ment and all other forms of authority. It was a great day to be an anarchist!

When we got to Anarchy House, it was packed. Nobody had come to have sex with the Clouds, but more than two hundred people had come to *see* who had come to have sex with them, and to talk about the demonstration. Because nobody would have sex with the Clouds, not even Jane and her boyfriends, they got petulant. In the end, they decided to lock themselves in my bedroom and have sex with each other. People just hung out in the living room and balcony talking about them having sex, imagining them sticking their skinny dicks in each other's scrawny orifices. I got very angry with Jane for letting them use my bedroom, but she was too stoned on ecstasy to care, so I went up and started banging on my door, screaming that I would kill them if they dirtied or broke anything. Just then, I heard a great crash and people started screaming that the cops had smashed the big window by the balcony and were coming in, dozens of them. People started running out the back door and jumping out windows. It was chaos!

I ran out back and jumped over the fence, crossed the neighbour's yard and got to the other side of the block. But it was my house, my room, so I went around the block and watched what was going on from the other side of the street. Punks and anarchists were escaping everywhere, and I saw the police lead the Clouds out, heads bloodied, in handcuffs. Next came Jane and Bob in handcuffs, and their eyes were glassy from all the ecstasy they had taken. The police loaded them in the van and they left. There were a few straggling punks in the street watching what was going on. I felt mad as hell at the police for smashing my house. I went up to one big bear of a cop with a bushy moustache and asked him what was going on.

He said, "There's a law against group sex in this city. We just broke up an orgy."

"What!" I said, "There were only three weird guys having sex privately in a back bedroom. Everybody else was just sitting and talking!"

"Three is enough. We're within the limits of the law."

"Why the hell did you break the win-dow?" I screamed.

"To get in the house, stupid!" He snarled back.

"But the door to that house is never locked. If you checked the door knob you would have known it wasn't necessary to damage the property!"

"It also wasn't necessary to burn your black flags and run around screaming like banshees to make the police look incompetent at Queen's Park!"

I yelled back, "So you're just doing this for revenge?"

He gave something between a snarl and a smirk and said, "Listening to freaks like you telling us that we should do whatever we want had its effect, didn't it, you stupid little punk. We're doing *exactly* what we want!"

I had no answer to that. I stood there stunned, remembering the guy who laughed like Satan and read Aleister Crowley. What he said suddenly rang so true it stung. Anarchy was perfectly all right for harmless and sedate anarchists, but a policeman, released of inhibi-tions and let loose on society was a dangerous wild beast. It was true!

Then the big cop I had been talking to turned to me and said, "We're going to get everybody else who lives at that place in cuffs, you know."

I walked away, fast, and when I was out of sight of the cops, I ran and I kept running until I was far away. I didn't even care when some losers in a Trans Am slowed down to scream that they were going to beat my head in as I hurried down Bloor Street West. So again, I had to abandon everything I owned, and I spent that night alone in a doughnut shop wasting what little money I had on coffee.

Chapter Four

I had no money, but by this time, I had plenty of punk rock friends, people who would let me sleep on their floor or sofa for a night or two. Steve and Ringo had the Terrible House of Sickness back together, and it had again become the same drunken chaotic party it had always been. But there was no way I was going back there, even for a night. It would be a nasty step backwards, and I didn't want to set a bad precedent. I started searching out invitations to sleep on different sofas every night. I was going from house to house for a week and I was beginning to wear out my welcome everywhere. I had to get a new place soon or be on the street again.

Anyway, I was at my friend Jennifer's house, Jennifer Ogilvie that is, the girl I met with Regan after the demonstration. She was one of those punk girls with long bleach blond hair teased into a rat's nest who always wore her Ramones tour shirt with piles of junky plastic and silver jewellery. We were listening to *Rocket to Russia,* when she told me about a girl she had met at a party named Jennifer Gould, who was a student at the Ontario College of Art. Jennifer Gould was looking for a roommate. She was so desperate to feel part of the scene, that she was willing to pay three-quarters of the rent. It was no problem; her parents were loaded, and she was from some small town up north, Hanover maybe, where the only industry was forestry. She had come to the big city of Toronto to escape the dullness.

It beat begging to sleep on a different floor or sofa every night, so I agreed to meet her. We invited her to a punk rock party at Jennifer Ogilvie's house and we talked. She was a short woman, and a bit fat. She had close-cropped black hair and a black leather jacket, but neither the hair nor the jacket made her stand out. She had that revolting fuckin' 'part-time punk' look about her. Her T-shirt looked as if it had been bought new off the shelf to wear at a party, no tears, no dirt, and no safety pins. Her leather jacket didn't have a single scrape. It shone like it was plastic.

The first thing Jennifer did after she introduced herself was to tell me about her art. She was interested in turning garbage into sculpture and said that she used part of the apartment as a studio. She wanted me as a friend and a roommate because she was impressed that I knew Blibber and The Rat Crushers personally. She asked me if I had slept with them. I said that I hadn't and asked her if she would kiss someone who had gargled a hamster. She seemed disappointed, but we talked more and became 'friends'. She asked me which punks I knew, and I told her they had all partied at the Terrible House of Sickness or Anarchy House at one time or another. She said nobody had told her about the Anarchist Picnic, so she didn't go. I told her that I had been there, and that it had been my bedroom the police had raided during the 'Orgy of the Clouds.'

When Jennifer heard that, she was desperate to be my friend and wouldn't let go of my arm all evening. I moved into her Queen Street apart-ment the next day.

I never felt close to Jennifer Gould. That's how it goes sometimes. You can know someone for years and never feel anything for them. We were like two strings of a guitar, out of tune with each other.

Her, I mean 'our,' apartment wasn't big. It was a large single room above a used clothing store on Soho near Queen Street. My bed was in one corner, and hers was in another. The rest of the room was taken up by a pile of junk she called her creative space, and there was a small sofa with TV and stereo near the door. There was a tiny kitchen in the back that was always a mess, but at least the bathroom was roomy. One of us could shower while the other did her make-up in front of the mirror. The studio corner was filled with cans, pieces of scrap metal and advertisements. Jennifer glued, stapled and nailed these together to create airplanes, cars, ships, guitars and other shapes to make her sculptures. Some of these works were seven feet long. When they were finished, I helped her carry them all the way to a storeroom at the Ontario College of Art just above Queen Street.

Jennifer said that if she could get the space she'd create life-size cars and even planes. She worked on her trash sculptures for hours and hours every afternoon and all through the weekend. I was still working as a waitress at the Golden Griddle in the afternoons and evenings, watching TV when I was at home in the day. We shopped for groceries together and cooked for each other. That was OK. She liked my pancakes and salad, and she made a good chicken curry. I started to regain the weight I had lost living at the Terrible House of Sickness and Anarchy House.

But that's about as far as I liked Jennifer Gould. Every time she talked to me, it was about what parties were coming up on the weekend. How the hell was I supposed to know? Living with her was off the scene, and I had to phone people to find out what was going on. Besides, if I went to a party, I wanted to go to get away from her, not to be with her as her doormat to 'cool punk rock society,' as she called it. I caught myself humming the Sex Pistols' version of *I'm not your Stepping Stone* a lot. However, I found her parties anyways, just to keep the relation-ship static.

One night we went to the new Terrible House of Sickness just around the corner from the old one. Steve had cut his mohawk off completely, but still had the goatee. You might have thought he had become a skinhead if you didn't know that he and Ringo had shaved their heads as a provocation. There were still a few Barf Puppies and glue sniffers to chase out of gigs. Steve's leather jacket and clothes were held together with even more safety pins and bike chains. He had set up the cage again in his bedroom. Ringo's clothes were even more threadbare. Drum keys and safety pins held his black leather jacket together. He was on PCP and breaking beer bottles on his head to show everybody that it didn't hurt. It was like old times, except I didn't belong there anymore, and I was embarrassed to be with Jennifer. She was just so uncool and smug and asked people all sorts of stupid questions about how they form-ulated the garbage of society into their 'punk rock lifestyle.' Nobody wanted to talk with her much.

There was a new girl, Dog's sister. Her punk rock name was Cat. Everybody called her Cat Morning Sickness. I said I was sorry her sister died. She said that she didn't care because she had never liked her anyway. After the bars closed, all the real punk rockers showed up, and Cat got really drunk and started running round all over the house with her pants off screaming that anyone with a condom could fuck her. I thought the night was so stupid that I just wanted to go home, but Jennifer thought it was cool just to be there, and I had to hang out with her because the trains and buses had stopped running and she was paying for the taxi home. It was awful.

The next weekend we went to Anarchy House. Jennifer insisted we show up early, over my protests that it was uncool to be anything but fashionably late. Only Jane and her creepy boyfriends lived there now, and when we got there, the place was empty. Most of the punks were at a Blibber show at Larry's Hideaway.

I noticed that the front window frame of Anarchy House was fixed so that you would never have known that half the Toronto police force had smashed their way into the house. The night of the raid, Jane and her boyfriends hadn't been at the police station longer than to be warned and fined. The Clouds had been fined too, and then they went back to Vancouver, getting on the four-day cross-country bus with two loaves of bread and a huge jar of peanut butter. Nobody had heard from them since. All I could think was that by the time they got to the West Coast they would stink as bad as I did when I came out of the park.

Then I tried to talk to Jane, but to her it was as if I had never existed. She was stoned on ecstasy again, and just stared at the wall or rubbed up against people. George didn't look like a punk anymore, despite his leather jacket with the Crass patch on back. He had grown his hair down to his shoulders. He started lecturing Jennifer about anarchy, and Jennifer tried to ask him about how he co-opted the garbage of society into his 'anarchist punk rock life style.' He stared at her as if she was speaking French or something and pretty soon, all the boyfriends did more ecstasy and retired to the bedroom to take turns poking their dicks into Jane. They left me alone in the living room with Jennifer, who didn't want to go home. She wanted to wait for the party to get started, but nobody came.

To kill time, I tried to tell Jennifer about how DOA was the most travelled band in Canada, and how they crossed the continent as if they were crossing town. But she didn't want to listen. We stayed awake in the living room listening to Crass and Dayglo Abortions records until four in the morning when we both fell asleep on the sofa.

After that, I found more parties and Jennifer asked people more stupid questions about how they recycled the garbage of their lives into their punk rock lifestyles. Being with her made me feel like a visitor on the punk rock scene, sick with myself because I was now nothing more than a part-time punk. When I suggested we stay home, drink beer, and watch TV, she got nasty and reminded me that she paid three quarters of the rent. I started calling up the Terrible House of Sickness in case Cat or Steve wanted to talk. I needed somebody, any-body but Jennifer Gould.

Another thing, Jennifer's taste in music really sucked. Or it didn't suck -- she just didn't understand anything. For example, she played David Bowie on the stereo a lot. Bowie's OK, he was a precursor to punk, but everybody, even parents, listen to him and he was such a main-stream sellout that he wasn't cool. You could see better than Bowie any night at the Rivoli Club where the Ontario College of Art bands like the Sturm Group or Vital Signs played. I suggested that we go see those bands because she might like the sound of timpanis played by bald art geeks on speed better than distorted guitars. She might recognize people from school, people with close-cropped hair and shiny leather jackets who only thought they were punks. Seeing them might even make her feel as if she belonged, and make her stop being my cling-on friend who begged me to help her meet interesting people. Jennifer just kept on talking about Bowie as if she was the only person who knew about him. For fuck's sake, he had sold hundreds of millions of records since the sixties. He wasn't exactly hot off the presses. Jennifer played Elvis Costello a lot, too. That was some-what OK. But what Jennifer couldn't understand was that Costello's music was too serious and made you feel depressed if you had a couple beers or were stoned. I played her the Sickness album and the bootleg tape of *Exploding Glue Heads*. I had an autographed copy of the Blibber and the Rat Crushers single, *I was a Teenage Hamster Killer*, but she couldn't see the value in these things because once she had met those people, they were no longer on a pedestal. She just didn't get it. Instead, she mumbled about turning the garbage of society into art as if she was above us all. I mean, if she wanted to meet the Rat Crushers and Sickness so badly, why couldn't she listen to them at home?

What really bugged me was when she got on the phone to her parents in Hanover. She talked like a princess. She rambled on about birthday presents for cousins or about when she was coming home to celebrate a fuckin' sappy Christmas. You know, maudlin old lady stuff. I told her about how I had told my mother and geeky stepfather Brad to fuck off because home was so oppressive and she looked at me as if I was shit. I mean, think about it; if my mother and Brad had had enough money to pay three quarters of the rent in an apartment for me in Toronto and send me to art school so I could glue, staple and nail garbage together and call it art, maybe I'd see things differently. But I still think I'd have some sympathy and understanding for people who didn't have that opportunity. But Jennifer was such a misery-shits rich brat she didn't see that.

I was supposed to spend all my free time searching out cool parties, but if some party happened at the Ontario College of Art, was I invited? No way, I just wasn't cool enough in that artsy way, so she'd just flat out tell me I wasn't invited. Then she'd get together on the phone with her best friend Cathy in Hanover and boast to her about all the cool places I'd taken her, not mentioning my name once. I got so mad I wanted to pull her fuckin' hair out.

But I didn't. I just quietly put up with it because I knew Jennifer paid three quarters of the rent, and that meant I had a place to stay.

Life went on like that, and soon it was winter. I told her that Steve Sickness once told me his big secret to being Toronto's premier punk party animal: he said it was no use searching out the party or looking all the time for something. You have to make the party yourself. So I told Jennifer that if she really wanted to be part of the party, we would have to make the party at our apartment.

Surprisingly, she saw the point, and we started to plan. I phoned everybody I knew, and Jennifer put out the money for a few cases of beer. We figured it would be best if thirty to fifty people showed up for the night because the apartment was small and we didn't want the line at the toilet to be too long. I spent a week calling people and getting the news around. Jennifer used some art materials to make up some invitation cards. I wrote the text, and we both spent an hour making up a hundred by hand. I thought the wording was clever:

Jennifer and Valerie are having a party!
Bring friends, but no crowds
-- and no Clouds! --

That was our party theme joke - NO CROWDS, NO CLOUDS - because people on the scene thought of the raid every time they heard my name.

Saturday night came, and of course, no-body arrived until the bars closed at one in the morning. We expected that, and even went out for a few drinks ourselves beforehand. Parties in Toronto are usually really boozecans of a sort and never get going until after one.

Soon, Jennifer Ogilvie, the punkette who had introduced us, showed up with Son of Sam, the band from Detroit who had played the Anarchist Picnic in Buffalo. It was their first time in Canada. They were big guys in black leather jackets and spiky hair. They were fun to talk to. I told them how much I liked their show in Buffalo, and they kept talking about how surprised they were that Canada was so much like the United States, and how weird it was to use money with the Queen on it rather than George Washington. They were in town looking for a place to book a gig. The singer was kind of cute, and I ended up kissing him on the sofa. We even snuck outside for a while and I put my hand down his pants. He was uncircumcised. But things didn't go further than that. Then we went back inside just as Steve and Ringo showed up with their dogs and six cases of beer to sell. They had closed the Terrible House of Sickness for the night to be with me. I was honoured. Blibber showed up and ate our magazines. Finally, Direct Action and the bouncers from Larry's Hideaway came in. It was turning into one fuckin' great party.

We listened to a tape of Detroit hardcore that Son of Sam brought, and they talked to Sickness about arranging a gig at Larry's. Eventually Ringo got stupid and started yelling at people. Then he got violent and smashed Jennifer's artwork, a six-foot airplane made out of Diet Pepsi cans. I thought there was going to be a scene, but she just laughed and said it was perfect now. I couldn't believe she was being so good-humoured. She said she would rename the sculpture after a famous plane crash and put it on display at the OCA art fair. She was drinking like a fish and, rather than asking people stupid questions about how they rearranged the garbage of society into their lives, she was talking about how much she'd like to visit Detroit. She was so drunk she tried to sing along with the Youth Youth Youth album. Everybody thought she was pretty funny. Then she threw up and passed out.

Everybody shuffled out by about four, and I was left checking damage. There was spilt beer and empty beer cans everywhere. The sofa was dirty from Direct Action putting their winter boots all over it, and there was a huge spot on the carpet where Jennifer had barfed. The only real damage was to Jennifer's art, and where Ringo had defaced our bathroom by writing the Sickness logo all over it with an industrial marker. I went to sleep with my head spinning from the beer, but thinking that maybe Jennifer and me were about to start a better relationship. I was genuinely happy for the first time in months.

Next morning I got up kind of groggy and for a few bad moments, I thought I was still living at the Terrible House of Sickness because I hadn't been so drunk since I lived there. The smell of stale beer, cigarettes, and puke was all so familiar. Then I remembered our party, and that I now lived with

Jennifer. I heard her clanging about in the kitchen, and thought of how much better we were going to get along.

I called out, "What are you doing in there?" She didn't answer, so I pulled myself out of bed and groped and stumbled into the kitchen to see what was going on. I got to the sink and Jennifer was there drinking water.

"Fifth glass," she said. "I've gotta get rid of this headache and get to work."

"What do you mean work? It's Sunday. You don't have school."

"I've got a new project. I'm going to photograph this whole apartment with its trash heaps of beer cans, cigarette butts, puke and other garbage and make a photo spread."

"Why?"

"Because I make art out of garbage. The photo spread is going to be called 'Trash Party Palace'. The whole project will take two or three days. I have to get the lighting I need, so don't touch a thing. I want it just the way it is, puke and all. The genuine article."

I didn't like the sound of that. The stale beer was already getting rancid. Even the Terrible House of Sickness was more hygienic.

I tried to compromise to keep us both happy. I said, "Couldn't I just rinse out all these cans and bottles for you, and you could make an airplane or something with them? The house is starting to stink."

"No!"

"What? Why are you getting mad?"

"You're not going to start getting in the way of my art. This is a once in a lifetime opportunity."

That was ridiculous, so I said "Once in a lifetime opportunity? Don't tell me you've never seen the aftermath of a beer drinking party before. Besides, you can photo the 'genuine article' at the Terrible House of Sickness anytime. It's always filthy like this the morning after, only they make a point of rinsing and dumping the cans first thing and swabbing the floor for beer and blood. I'm sure Steve and Ringo would let you photograph their place. Besides, I live in this house too, and I don't want to live with the mess, especially the stale beer and puke."

Jennifer started to get very angry and raised her voice. "No! I'm the artist, and since it was my party, I, in a sense, created it. If I went to the Terrible House of Sickness to do it, it would be journalism, and I'm not a journalist, I'm an artist. Let me remind you, little garbage heap Valerie, it's my apartment! I only let you live here. If you don't like it, I can get my parents to pay your quarter of the rent and you're out on the street. Now leave the mess as it is!"

"Hey, I've paid my rent for the month."

"My father's name is on the lease and the landlady thinks there's only one person living here, and if you don't want to live here, I'll get the police to remove an unwanted guest."

Then she went back to drinking water.

I was so angry that I walked out and kept walking around the city all day. There was no answer to what she said. Dammit, how did being born so lucky give her the right to be unreasonable and selfish?

The garbage, even the puke, stayed until Tuesday, and I put up with the smell, but didn't talk to Jennifer much. She got some art nerds from the OCA in with lighting and she took pictures: the sink full of smashed glass, the beer-soaked sofa cushions, the heaps of cans in the corner, her smashed airplane and even the defaced bathroom. The guy who did the lighting brought a beer, and when he was finished, he threw the can onto one of the piles. Jennifer got mad at him and removed it saying that it wasn't part of the 'genuine article.' How ridiculous can you get? I think anybody who took Jennifer's art seriously must be mentally retarded.

There's enough garbage around anyway, who needs to go to an art gallery to see more of it? Fuck, I don't know. Maybe Jennifer's right and the artists can make art out of any material they like, even garbage. But I still say you're not Picasso just because you put some pile of beer cans on display and call it art. You still got to be good, you've still got to be interesting.

When the photo shoot was over, I asked Jennifer if we could clean it up, she said she was going out for coffee with the OCA lighting guy, but that I could clean it up if I liked. They left and I got to cleaning. It took me four hours to get everything straight, and she didn't come back to help. She didn't even say thank you or answer me when I asked her if I'd get an acknowledgement when she presented the photos. She just laughed at me as though I had asked a very stupid question.

Life continued as usual the rest of the week. Saturday came, and I said I'd rather give the parties a rest this week because of all the excitement last week. She agreed with me on that. Then we talked about the graffiti in the bathroom. She said she'd go out and get some-thing from the art supply to scrub the industrial marker off the tiles.

I stayed at home and watched TV. It was about six by the time Jennifer got back. Instead of bringing some kind of solvent, she had a few rolls of wallpaper, paste, bucket and roller. She unrolled one of the rolls and said, "So Valerie, I've decided that it'll be easier to wallpaper than to clean off the felt marker. How do you like the paper?"

I couldn't answer, but stood there looking dumb with my mouth open. She had chosen that same fuckin' wallpaper my mother had, the one with the stupid looking wooden beavers!

So I raised my voice, "No! My mother has that same wallpaper with those stupid beavers. That's what drove me out of home. Leave the beer cans piled up stinking forever, but don't you think I'll ever look at walls with that ugly beaver stuff on it!"

She decided to put me in my place. "I don't care if you've got complexes about your mother. That's your problem, not mine. Do you understand? I like the beavers, I paid for the wallpaper and it's my apartment. If you don't like it, you can leave."

Then it all came out. I started screaming about how she was mistaken if she thought she was, oh, so much better than me just because she was lucky enough to be born with a nice rich mommy and daddy who gave her money, were emotionally supportive and paid the bill for her to play with trash. It just showed that she was trash herself if she used that privilege to bully me, making me live and sleep with the heaps of stinking beer cans, puke, and her insults. And now this stupid wooden beaver wallpaper? What kind of art student was she if she had no better taste than a suburban housewife from Etobicoke? So what if I had complexes about my mother? I certainly wouldn't have forced something like that on her if it upset her.

She got all smarmy and started yelling back trying to sound superior to lowly little Valerie. She said I was right, that I had better not put up anything on the wall that upset her, but that since it was her apartment she would put up anything that damn well pleased her. Then she started going on about how she didn't need me as a roommate and her father would pay the rent. She said I was shit because I didn't even know where my father was, and besides I was dirt like my divorced mother. Divorces just didn't happen in her family and–

I smacked her.

I smacked her so hard across the face they must have heard it two kilometres away at the yuppie bars on the harbour front. I didn't even think about it. I never thought I would ever say a word in defence of my mother to anybody, but now I had smacked a rich bitch to save her honour. I mean, my mother treated me poorly, but anybody could end up in a bad marriage. Maybe I was confused about my feelings, but not as confused as Jennifer was. She just stood there, eyes glassy with shock. Then she slumped to the floor and started crying hysterically, and begging me not to kill her. What kind of garbage did she think I was that I might kill her? I finally saw what a stupid fuckin' bitch she was.

I was suddenly cool headed and rational. I said, "Go on. Put up your fuckin' wallpaper. I don't care. I'm out of here at the end of the week. I'm going out tonight. We need to spend some time apart."

Then I gathered some things in my back-pack and walked out. I walked to Osgoode Station, and the only thing I could think of was how I had become like the Little Fadette, the girl in the French novel, defending her mother's honour in the face of privileged brats. At the subway, I made some phone calls. Mohawk Suzy was having a party at her house and I took the subway to where she lived near Kipling Station and waited on her steps until the bars closed and punks started arriving. She had an amazing party, and half of punk Toronto was there. Suzy gets along with everyone.

Anyways, it turned out that members of a 'new wave' band called K were there. New punks thought they were dorky, but everybody knew that K were old punks, so it was OK to party with them. Mohawk Suzy and her friends said they had some kind of record deal with Capitol Records or EMI Canada. I got into a conversation with Dave the Cat, their guitarist. He still wore his old leather jacket. He had removed the studs, but that made it even more worn. He had hair a little longer than your average Toronto punk, but nothing longer than DOA. I asked what K stood for, and he told me that nobody knew, not even the band. I told him I didn't believe him, and started tickling him so he would tell me, but he tickled me back because he was stronger, and soon after that, we were kissing and I told him all about my troubles with my roommate Jennifer. Everyone called him Dave the Cat 'cause he was really skinny and made all sorts of funny slinky moves when he played. I had met him before, but tonight he suddenly seemed really cute.

Before the party was over, I had an invitation from Dave and the other members of the band to move into Heartbreak Hotel, that was what they had named their warehouse practice space. I accepted the offer just because I had the feeling that despite the little problems that might come up, I'd get more respect than I would at Jennifer's. We partied all night listening to music and drinking beer. I never slept, and when the sun came up, I went back to the apartment and told Jennifer I was moving out and she nodded. I didn't tell her where I was going and she didn't ask. She cowered in the kitchen as if she still thought I would kill her. I just walked out the door with my black leather jacket, my hockey bag of clothes, a few records and said, "See you around sometime."

I never saw her again.

Chapter Five

So I moved into the Heartbreak Hotel and I finally got fucked. The day I moved in, Dave put me up against the wall in the bedroom and fuckin' gave it to me. I clung to the coat rack and moaned as he pulled my jeans off and slid inside me. Afterward, I had all these feelings that I never had before. I felt I could love Dave forever and I was dazzlingly optimistic about the future.

Like I said, the Heartbreak Hotel was the live-in and practice space for K. Dave the Cat had told me the truth; nobody ever knew what the K stood for. They had just chosen to use the letter K as the name of their band 'cause they could never agree on a name. There were three other guys in the band besides Dave. They all dressed pretty much the same, but they wore sunglasses all the time, so you couldn't tell if they were punks or the Blues Brothers.

Everybody called Dave the Cat by his full nickname. So it was always, 'Dave the Cat this' or, 'Dave the Cat that' when people were talking to him. His real name was David Braun. The other guys were Greg, Bob and Elliot. Dave and I shared a bedroom and the other guys had separate rooms. Greg slept in the practice space behind the drums, even though it was cold and damp. He was weird.

The only drawback to the Heartbreak was that Elliot and Bill would find these fifteen-year-old sluts and keep them at the Heartbreak for a few days until the little runaways got scared and went home to mom and dad. I don't know where they picked up the little bitches in black spandex and pink headbands that looked like groupies for Devo. Daycare maybe? I was nervous the police would show up and charge somebody with statutory rape or something. But I didn't care, as long as the little sluts didn't eat my food.

K lived together, but they only practiced on weekends. That was the only time they didn't work different shifts. There was always some-body practicing guitar riffs or a new drum beat in the rehearsal space, so the house was full of music. I became something like the mother of the house. Those guys cooked, but not anything like real food. They made bachelor food: pizza toast, spaghetti, sometimes hamburgers or tuna sandwiches with too much mayonnaise. I cooked up some real stuff that I had learned to make while working at the Golden Griddle: apple pancakes with back bacon and caesar salads, but no fuckin' boiled cabbage. Also, I picked up a lot of beer bottles to make the place acceptable for human habitation.

So you want to be a rock star? Do you want to know what kind of shit K had to put up with? K had a development deal with Capitol Records. I know this sounds like a dream come true, but it was really a kind of death. What happens in a development deal is that the record company gives the band something like 5000 bucks to pay for expenses for a couple of years, and the band has to sign a contract not to sign with anybody else. Of course, nothing ever comes of it, and the band is paralysed and can't move their career forward unless the record company decides that they are the lucky one out of a hundred bands that they will turn into rich and famous rock stars. They couldn't even play any of the usual bars, just a few places on a hard-to-book circuit that Capitol Records approved of. K took the 5000 bucks and used it to pay for their practice space and guitar strings. They were dreamers.

I told Dave again and again that he had signed away his future and his band to a dead end, and that they should change the name and play for money under a different name. Fuck, it had been eight months since they had last seen Capitol Record's agent. Dave just smiled and said that it was all part of the rock 'n' roll life-style. He got jobs washing dishes, packing boxes in warehouses and being a security guard. None of his jobs lasted more than three or four weeks. After six months, he quit working completely and went on Unemployment Insurance. That meant that we had to use what little money we scrimped together from his UI checks and the money from my job serving breakfast at The Golden Griddle to pay our share of the rent. We couldn't go anywhere or have fun because we couldn't even afford the price of beer at a bar, so we drank at the Heartbreak and scraped by. We had to give up the deluxe pancakes and caesar salads and eat only macaroni and cheese. Sometimes we didn't even have that because one of Elliot or Greg's little sluts would sneak into the cupboard and eat what we had. I preferred that Dave work, but I didn't want to be the sort of bitch girlfriend that does a lot of nagging.

So life went on, and despite the little problems, I was happy to be somewhat domesti-cated, almost married. There was no violence like at the Terrible House of Sickness or belittle-ment like when I lived with Jennifer. I even grew my hair long and wore peasant dresses around the house. This was considered cool by the older punks because you weren't really an older punk yourself until you started rebelling against punk a bit. It even gave you a bit of a mystique with the younger punks.

It was cool to be the girlfriend of one of the members of K because they were old punks. All of them had played with the Viletones, Diodes, Forgotten Rebels or Screaming Sam at some point. K didn't play live often because of their development deal, but when they did play, a few old punks, people in their twenties, came to see them. People even came back from shows to hang around the house. It was still cool, and I was still somebody visible on the scene. We even sold some beer and pot to pay the rent.

Only thing I didn't like about Dave was some of his asshole friends; even Elliot and the other guys in K grumbled about them. What used to happen was that various 'old friends', wherever they came from, used to show up without invitation at around two in the morning. There were usually about five or six in the group, although they weren't always the same people. Mostly a bunch of chain-smoking rocker types. They'd bring three or four cases of beer and some pot. Dave just couldn't say no to partying till dawn any night of the week. None of these losers ever spoke much. They just sat there tipping up their beer bottle to their mouths and deciding what record cover they'd use to roll a joint. I sat with them once or twice, but they were all too creepy and silent. They listened to The Byrds, Led Zeppelin, old Rolling Stones, Frank Zappa, the Vibrators, prehistoric rock.

Dave couldn't explain who these guys were to me except to say they were the people he always drank with and that he'd just met them 'along the way'. I asked him to ask them to come over less often, but he got irritated with me.

So it went on, whenever any of these guys got a welfare or Unemployment Insurance check, there would be three or four nights of Dave staying up with them, and me wishing the creeps would go away.

Time went on and I got my shit more together. I put what I could save from the money I got waitressing and Dave's UI checks in the bank, and three or four months later, we had enough money to move into our own little apartment not too far from the Heartbreak so it would still be convenient for Dave to practice. Now Elliot and Bill's little sluts couldn't eat our food. I even convinced Dave to calm down his rock 'n' roll lifestyle a little, and he promised he would never invite any of his loser friends to spend the night at the apartment. He doubled his effort to do something to make our relation-ship more stable and got his old job as a security guard back.

I was now eighteen and felt quite mature after all the shit I'd been through. In a year, it would be legal for me to drink, and I even started to look at finishing high school by taking night courses. That would take two years to complete, but I did not intend to stay a waitress forever. Dave was my man, and having him around the house made me feel happy. It was fine that my mother and Brad had their little piece of heaven, now Dave and I would have ours. I began to dream that Dave and I would get married, have children; that he'd join a real working blues band and bring in some money, that I'd get through high school and get a job in an office that paid good money and that we could settle down into a real life.

By October, I thought it was time that I asked Dave what he thought of a family. I didn't mean I wanted one like tomorrow, I was thinking about the long term. I mean, one day I was going to be twenty-five, right? He said he didn't want to talk about it, and I said I did. I came on too strong and started nagging, maybe. He stormed out and spent the night at the Heartbreak. His loser friends came over and he ended up drinking until dawn. That meant he couldn't get to work the next day and they fired him from his security guard job. I let that go by, but told him he'd better be getting a new job or we'd have money problems soon. But he just started calling up his buddies and spending two or three nights a week at the Heartbreak. I didn't know what else to do. I didn't want our nice life to go to hell, so I spoke to him softly. I tried to talk him back into being responsible. I told him that there were many security companies out there, and he could take his choice. I reminded him that he had made a commitment when he moved in with me, and I, for one, would almost rather live in the street than go back and live with the little macaroni-stealing sluts at Heartbreak. He promised to try harder and started to look for work. I felt things were getting back on track.

One day while Dave was out at a job interview, I got this letter.

Dear Valerie,

We don't want to tell you our names, but we know you and want to do you a favour. Dave the Cat is shit. His name is not Dave the Cat. We called him Dave the Loser or Dave the Fuck-Up. You are cool and pretty. He is ugly and a freak. People who thought you were cool are laughing at you. Dave the Loser never had a girlfriend before because he's weird. He can't talk to women. The only people he relates to are his loser welfare buddies. He is almost thirty. For more than twelve years, he's been sitting up every night with his loser friends until the eyes bug out of his head. They don't even talk because they're too stupid. Dave the Fuck-up doesn't talk either, because he's one of them. They laugh weird at stupid things. They're creepy because they sound like hyenas. The only girlfriend Dave the Loser ever had was Jane Blaud. You don't know her. She lives in Winnipeg now. We call Jane Blaud 'Jane Bloodsucker'. She is a bitch. Dave the Fuck-up never got fucked until he met her. He used his credit card to buy her everything. Dave the Fuck-up was so stupid he went along with it. She didn't even work. She got him to buy her a refrigerator and stereo and a dozen dresses. Dave the Fuck-up was too stupid to realize he was being used. Everybody was laughing at him. Jane Bloodsucker was laughing at him too and made fun of him behind his back. When Dave the Loser reached his debt limit, she wanted to get rid of him. She decided to humiliate him. One night at the Terrible House of Sickness Dave was drinking till he was stupid as usual, and Bloodsucker went down on Steve and Asshole in Steve's cage and left the bedroom door open so everybody could see. It wasn't Steve and Asshole's fault. They didn't know she was Dave's girlfriend. When somebody told him what was going on, he passed out. Then Bloodsucker left town and Dave went to live with the K. They are losers too. You're the only other woman Dave the Loser had. Now everybody is laughing at you. Dump the Loser for your own good. We are your friends, not your enemies. There are eight of us, but we don't want to sign our names.

Sincerely,

Eight Anonymous Friends

When I finished reading the letter, I was mad. I thought it was some of the bitches who hung around the Terrible House of Sickness. Guys couldn't write to get under a girl's skin like that. I wanted to tear their hair out and break their heads. I didn't give a damn about Bloodsucker. How dare a bunch of little bitches, who probably just want to be locked in Steve's cage, try to destroy my relationship? I went to the bathroom and punched the wall and cried and bit my hands until they bled because I was so mad. I didn't even hear Dave come in. I had left the letter on the kitchen table, and while I was crying in the bathroom, Dave came in and read it. Then he started banging the bathroom door and screaming, "What the fuck is this! What the fuck is this!" I came out and tried to hug him and explain how mad I was, but he had the wrong idea. He thought that I thought he was shit. He wouldn't listen to me. He threw me aside and started screaming it wasn't true and that I was a stupid bitch. I tried to tell him that's not how it was, and that I thought the letter was a lie, but he wouldn't listen. He took his skinny arm and hit me hard in the face so I had a bleeding nose, and I went crazy with screams and crying. I ran back to the bathroom crying in hysterics because my life was fucking up. Dave picked up his guitar and amplifier and went back to the Heartbreak. He left me alone with all those bills to pay.

I pulled myself together by the evening. I wasn't going to get thrown out of my apartment until the end of the month, because that's when the rent was due. So I went to work for a few days and everything was normal, except I was crying whenever I was alone. I had to take a few days to figure out what to do. I didn't have enough money for the rent, but I had enough for food. I decided to go to the Heartbreak Hotel to talk to Dave.

When I got there, he was hungover, looked pale, and didn't want to talk. I went back a couple of days later and it was just the same. Elliot and the other band members told me Dave the Cat was drinking and staying up every night. I let it pass for a few more days. Once I phoned in the middle of the night because I knew he would be up partying, and he told me to fuck off. I heard all those guys he was with laughing in the background.

I went to my landlord and asked him if I could pay half the rent for the next month and then the rest in a few weeks time. He grumbled, but agreed. That was a relief. But I still had to get Dave back, and I was throwing up in the mornings, so I went to see the doctor. She ran some tests and a few days later, she told me I was pregnant.

What was my reaction? I don't care what anybody says, but I was happy. I mean, it's natural isn't it? Even if people consider it inconvenient. Inconvenient for what? I was never treated as anything but an inconvenience. But people shouldn't be treated as inconveniences. People are people, even babies. They can't help it. I wanted to tell Dave, but I didn't know how to tell him anything. I thought he'd be happy. I thought this would give him something to live for. I stayed up late a couple of nights trying to think of some way to tell him. I couldn't think of anything better than, "Dave, I'm pregnant."

I went to the Heartbreak Friday night, just because I knew everybody would be up and drinking and in a good mood. But when I walked in the door, the guys were looking down at the floor. They were drinking beer and Dave was nowhere around. Even Elliot looked away from me. He was on the phone telling some little slut not to come over because something terrible had come up.

I didn't know what to make of that. Finally, I said, "Where's Dave?"

Greg, he was the drummer, looked at me, and said, "I'd like to talk to you outside."

We went out into the street and he took me around the corner into a back alley. There was a pile of old tires there.

"Sit down," he said.

"Why?"

"Just sit down."

So we sat down and he heaved a deep sigh as if he was about to cry, and I began to think the worst had happened.

I said, "What is it?"

"Dave is d...dead."

"What!"

"He died in his sleep. The doctor says it was a heart attack, but it won't be official until after the autopsy."

I was crying already. "What happened? Was he doing coke or something?"

"Maybe that will come out in the autopsy, but even if he was, you and me know it's not what killed him. It was staying up late all night every night for his rock 'n' roll lifestyle. Not sleeping, not eating right, living off beer. It takes its toll. Dave wasn't strong physically. He was a skinny guy."

So I cried for a while and went back into the house with Bill, where the guys from the band were looking very depressed. Once in a while, someone would cry. It wasn't much of a wake, and I wanted to be alone, so I went home and cried by myself.

Everyone was understanding -- for about a week. K borrowed a fill-in guitarist from a band called The Animal Stags, and they played a memorial show for Dave the Cat at the Beverly Tavern. Only about a dozen people came. After that, nobody spoke of Dave much. The autopsy didn't report anything beyond a bit of marijuana in his system and a lot of alcohol, but not enough that it should have killed him. The report just said that he had a weak heart and a weak constitution.

I thought the turnout at the Beverly was fuckin' pathetic. People on the scene who had been listening to his guitar playing for years should have paid a bit more respect to his memory. OK, he wasn't a genius, but he was damned good. I know he was a quiet type. He didn't use words; he spoke with his guitar. If he had been a loudmouth hell-raiser, maybe people on the scene would have remembered him better. But maybe that's all that counts, being a loudmouth hell-raiser.

About a week after Dave the Cat died, Brat X, the bass player from the Rent Boys, that over-rated bunch of male prostitutes that played pseudo-disco and called themselves funk-punk fusion, threw himself in front of a van just because he was depressed about something. But just because he had been a loudmouth and showed up at everybody's parties with a Union Jack tied around his elbow and talked all the time in a fake British accent, people went on mourning him for months. The guy could barely play his instrument compared to Dave. Brat X's friends even made up this story that he had hung himself because it seemed a more romantic end than impulsively throwing himself into traffic. Everybody knew the truth because it had been whispered all around, but aloud, nobody said that Brat X had thrown himself in front of a van. There were even some friends of the Rent Boys who got in touch with a spiritualist and sat around in a circle on heroin holding each other's hands trying to get in touch with Brat X on the other side.

I was so disgusted that I stopped coming around the clubs or the parties, and just started living my own life. I still have friends, mostly old punks or ex-punks who don't hang around much. I decided not to get an abortion. I'm no anti-abortionist or anything; I just don't want to do that to my body. I got in touch with Dave's parents. They let me come to the funeral, but didn't want anything to do with me after that. I told them it was their grandchild, but they didn't care. They just looked at me as if I'd been responsible for Dave's death and walked away. I wanted to tell them how I had been the only one trying to get Dave out of his rock 'n' roll lifestyle habits, but they didn't want to listen.

I still have his guitar, a white Fender Stratocaster. Nobody will take that away. Maybe I'll have Elliot teach me to play Dave's riffs one day if I have the time.

The baby's coming in a month. I have a feeling it will be a girl. I managed to keep the apartment because I'll get maternity benefits when I leave my job.

So what about the future? I don't know. When the baby comes, I'll take care of her as best I can. It'll be tough. She'll have a tough life. Maybe I'll get married or have a live-in boyfriend like my mother. The thing that scares me is that one day she might walk out at sixteen as I did. I'll let her have a say about the wall-paper and not force her to eat only the things I like. I promise!

The End of the Human Race

A science fiction short story

by

Stewart Black

Jack Starr was a handsome but lonely young man of twenty-eight without a girlfriend. He hated to admit it, but like everybody else on Planet Earth in the year 2025 CE, he would have to hunt for a mate on a dating site on the World Wide Web. Social media had all but wiped out parties and social events for his generation. Well, as long as he was going to sort through pictures and vids of girls he would switch off the small screen of his computer and attach the keyboard to the wall-sized high definition monitor that he used for his job as a freelance photo editor. A short search and he signed up to 'Out of this World Dating.' Sign up took only a few minutes and an old style email address, some personal information such as his hobbies and the uploading of his most narcissistic selfie photos; the attraction was that there was no charge to his credit account unless there was a successful hook-up. Dating guaranteed!

A few minutes later he was looking at the profiles of mulatto girls and any other women that seemed to him exotic. Most had waists that pulled in very tightly in the bikini shots, shaped like hour-glasses!

'They're all too perfect,' he thought. 'There really is a lot of photo touch up here. Is there nobody honest about who they really are?'

The introductory messages were often quite infantile. Susan X, a slightly chubby one hiding her size behind a fuzzy sepia photo effect, introduced herself thus,

> 'Cute Donna Summer look-alike searching for her white man. "I feel love." Enjoys chases around the coffee table, hugs and movies. No rap music… Pleeeze!'

According to Susan X's information she had signed up eight months ago. Well, if she was still searching, there was some problem. She was either too crazy to date or had bad hygiene. He'd give that one a skip.

Jack sighed and continued to scroll through profiles. There were a lot of 'Donna Summers' out there.

The next profile gave him a shock. The profile photo was of an olive green face with turquoise blue eyes that were too big and round to be human and straight turquoise hair that fell over bare green shoulders. The nose was inhumanly small, and the smile through her dark green lips showed large and slightly canine teeth. The tiny chin came almost to a point that made her seem to pout. Still, she was cute to look at, in the way that cartoon girls were always cute to look at.

'Don't they have filters to get rid of jokers like this,' he said aloud.

Still, he clicked on the profile. A full photo set! The bikini shots were of her standing smiling in what looked like a spaceship control centre made of brown organic material oozing turquoise fluid and control knobs that looked like octopus tentacles. Her legs were too long for a member of the human race: she had six long toes on each foot and looked fantastic in stilettos. She had no belly button and was svelte in her waist. Her name was Cauda Draconis. Her breasts looked human enough, besides being green, and stood out ample and firm. If only she were real! He read the introduction.

> 'Non-smoker member of Alien Species and one woman planetary invasion force seeks earth man for love and romance. Enjoys reading, chases around the coffee table, hugs and movies. No rap music. No drug addicts, please!'

According to her profile she had joined thirty seconds ago!

Jack looked again at the photos. He was an expert at detecting fakes: he had taken many courses as part of his training as a photo site editor, and something about these, perhaps it was the shadows, looked real. Perhaps it was the sloppiness of the object that looked like a coffee cup that had spilled its oozing turquoise contents over the control tentacles in the background. Perhaps it was that steak knife with the alien symbols on the handle that seemed to have fallen out of the cup. At least she didn't like rap music, always a good thing.

The chat window opened up.

'Do you really think I'm sexxxy? I can come from orbit and be with you in thirty of your earth minutes.'

Flippantly, and without thinking, he typed back.

'Certainly, and if you really are an alien your advanced tracking systems will allow you to find my address without my giving it to you. Love and kisses. See you in thirty minutes. Jack.'

The reply came too quickly. In fact the very instant he pushed the return on his keyboard.

'See you in thirty, my delicious one. XXX.'

Jack logged off and shut down the wall screen. Something bugged him about this joker. He did not like being made a fool of. He could go another day without a girlfriend. He started thinking about logging a complaint with Out of this World Dating. He had little enough free time as it was without dealing with such nonsense. He set about getting some work done at home. He flipped the wall screen back on. So many old photos to scan through for the company. So many images that could or could not be sold and licensed. That was his contract. He made the decisions about which images from ancient photo albums that 'Family Photos for Cash,' his current employer, should or should not buy for their photo bank.

For some reason he paused from his work and got up to brush his teeth and hair. Not his usual thing to do at this hour, seven in the evening. He felt silly. It was as if he really were expecting the cute olive green girl in the very clever photo fake to turn up at his door. He sat back down and began tagging a set of photos of children on the beach from the 1960's as uninteresting and unacceptable.

Suddenly the lights dimmed and flickered, and there was a loud whooshing or whirring sound outside that rattled the windows of his house. The clock widget on his screen read exactly 7.30. Three soft knocks on the door. He shivered.

'All coincidence. This all has an explanation,' he said aloud.

He quickly cleared the mess of coffee cups from the table in front of the sofa, feeling silly for doing so, and rushed to the door. He checked his hair in the wall mirror as though his date were really showing up and felt even sillier. Heart pounding, he took a deep breath and opened the door.

It was her. She was shorter than she had seemed in the photos. Perhaps five-foot two inches. But there she was with her olive green face, inch and a half wide eyes and turquoise blue hair falling over her shoulders. Her dark green lips formed into a kissable little pout. She wore a long purple robe decorated with alien symbols. A flying saucer the size of a small car glowed red from the heat of entry into the earth's atmosphere in Jack's driveway. A breeze came toward the house and he could feel the heat waft up from the space ship even here in the doorway.

'Greetings, earthling,' she said in a soft unaccented voice and smiled, showing off those cute canine teeth. 'We thought we would start the planetary invasion with a home invasion. May I come in?'

What could he do?

'Of course,' he said.

She paused in her step.

'Oh, let me take care of that,' she said pointing to the flying saucer. 'I just wanted to show it off.' She snapped two of her six long fingers and it disappeared. 'Invisibility shield,' she said, as she stood on her toes to kiss him on the cheek.

Her kiss felt warm and wet and very welcome. Jack wondered if he had gone mad and were hallucinating. If so, it was pleasant to be mad. He may as well enjoy it.

She stepped through the door, shutting it softly but securely, her purple robe patterned with alien symbols flapping about her. She began gently pushing Jack back into the living room and speaking so fast that he could hardly follow what she said. She didn't even allow him time to offer her something to drink. What did alien women drink anyway?

'I'm so glad you let me in willingly. This makes matters so much more convenient. I'm Cauda Draconis, but you can call me Cauda. That's Latin for Dragon's Tail. I'll call you Jack. Let's not waste time beating around the bush as your English expression has it. My species has a single ship in low orbit around your planet. It's cloaked and cannot be detected by your technology. You would not like to be there. We are huge amoeba-like creatures living in tubs of sticky turquoise liquid and clouds of ammonia gas at temperatures above 150 degrees centigrade. We are DNA based life forms like you. We have been space borne for so many millions of years that we no longer know our home planet, but we come from the direction of the constellation of Hercules. You may call us Herculeans. When we need to get something done we grow specialised appendages that we call "animals." These separate to take on a life of their own and create "machines" and whatever else we need. I am one of these appendages, although I am a very specialised and unique project. Further surgery and gene modification became necessary at several stages of my development. I was created from our flesh during a period of ten of your earth years. I was brought up in the low pressure, low temperature oxygen chamber with the control tentacles that you saw in the bikini shots. I hope you find me irresistible. My parent becomes angry when I do not clean up my "coffee cups," but I do not care. I was created for life on earth and contact with your species. I am very happy to be here on earth. I feel that I am at home. I have never met another humanoid and I am so happy to meet one at last that I could cry. I have been very lonely growing up in the laboratory on the ship. I have been educated so as to fit in with your cultural group and I particularly like reading Balzac. My favourite film is Jaws.'

Cauda kissed him again and softly pushed Jack toward the sofa. She talked even faster.

'We Herculeans think in terms of pure geometry and are conscious on several levels that you are unaware of. Don't even ask. It would be like explaining the differential calculus to a dog.

I hated it when my parent made me watch those stupid episodes of Star Trek as part of my cultural training. Warp factor six… ridiculous! Faster than light travel is impossible and humanoids only exist here on earth. It takes us many tens of thousands of your earth years to travel between star systems on generation ships. Many generations live and die in the passage. Invasion and species assimilation can take even longer, that is if we are lucky enough to encounter sentient life forms…. Oh, and the big bang theory is wrong. What your scientists see as the beginning of the universe is only a minor local phenomenon. I love you.'

Then she threw her two bare olive green arms around him and gave Jack the tightest and most constricting hug he had ever had. She was warmer than an earth woman and her scent was of musk mingled with something as subtle and sweet as ambergris. She smelled very pleasant.

Cauda pressed one long green finger to his lips to keep him quiet and continued softly into his ear as she hugged him, pressing him always more closely, like a boa constrictor enfolding its prey.

'We Herculeans also have a sense of humour. Believe it or not, humour is common to all intelligent life forms in our galaxy. We are slightly amused but deeply offended by your cornball, badly dated and monotonously repetitious science fiction that has hardly progressed since H.G. Wells and his book about legions upon legions of horrible little green men invading your planet. That is why the council of those that spawned me decided that it would be hilariously ironic and most efficient if the invasion were carried out by one very very nice little green woman.'

Cauda had begun wrapping her rather serpentine, but very warm, green legs around him. She paused from her light speed talk, opened the turquoise pupils of her eyes even more widely and for a moment seemed deeply concerned about how Jack was taking all this.

'You do think I'm nice, don't you?' she said in a very soft and pleading voice.

'Why, yes,' Jack said, and he was telling the truth. He did like her, even if his planet were being invaded.

She smiled, showing those sharp white teeth.

'Oh, I'm the happiest girl in the whole galaxy. I was so worried you might not like me. Don't you think the flying saucer was a nice touch?'

She kissed him on the lips and he felt a salty but pleasant taste, like olives, in her saliva.

'But why me?' he asked.

'You were good looking and you were new. Out of this World Dating was full of people who had been signed up for eight months or more. If you can't find a date in that time you are either too crazy to date or have bad hygiene.'

How did she know the exact words that gone through his head as he had viewed the profiles of all those 'Donna Summers?'

'That makes sense,' he said. 'But why didn't you contact some government?'

Cauda laughed, 'Don't take me to your leader, earthling. He's horrible! Really, really horrible!'

Jack laughed too. So alien life forms really did have a sense of humour!

'Now, we don't have time to waste,' she said.

Cauda stood back and let the robe drop. She was naked but for her stilettoes, and even more beautiful than in her photos with her flat stomach and her firm breasts with pointy green nipples like ripe avocadoes. She was beginning to sweat or rather to exude something sweet smelling like sweat all over her body. Jack knew all too well what was happening. She was exuding something like human female sexual hormones, but ten thousand times more powerful. He had to use all his self-control to keep himself from trying to screw her right there on the coffee table. Cauda was a tease. Jack lost his self-control. He jumped at her, she leapt from him and ran around the coffee table giggling as he tried again and again to grab her.

Cauda was now laughing like a maniac, 'Resistance is futile, earthling. Prepare for a close encounter of the third kind!'

♀ W ♀

They lay in bed.

The soft light seeped into the bedroom from the wall screen in the living room. Somehow electric light seemed romantic.

'I'm the first human to have screwed an alien,' said Jack Starr and laughed. 'That was the best sex I have ever had. Human women cannot ride a man like that!'

Cauda Draconis's smile turned to a frown. She stopped running her six long fingers gently up and down his chest.

Offended by the chauvinisticly male coarseness of his remark, she retorted, 'Well, I hope I am much more to you than one small step for man!'

'I love you,' he said apologetically.

The smile returned to her little green mouth and she purred like a kitten, 'I love you too, sweetheart, my delicious one.'

He pulled her warm green body close and continued, 'I started to love you when you mentioned Balzac and Jaws. I mean, why would your species go through so much trouble if you had come here to eat us alive?'

'Well, now that you mention it…' she said, baring her canine teeth and forcing his neck into the pillow with her surprisingly strong hands. She sank her teeth into the arteries in his neck like Dracula in the old movies. Somehow Jack was paralyzed and he could feel himself sinking away into nothingness as Cauda greedily drew in the blood that ran from his heart and should have supplied his brain with oxygen. As she satiated herself on his life force all became dark. He was not religious, but said a brief prayer to his maker thanking him that as he was about to die, it was at least at the hands of somebody he liked…

♀ **W** ♀

Jack Starr felt weak. He had just come to. The clock by the bed read 9.30 pm. He had been unconscious for half an hour.

Cauda Draconis was still naked and straddled his chest.

'But I'm still alive,' he managed to whisper.

'I am here to eat you alive, not dead,' she explained. 'Your morbid species has such a hang-up about eating dead things. We eat the living. Don't worry. You've lost a pint of blood, and you get more in return than you would get from those profiteering vampires at the Red Cross. Do you feel hungry?'

'Why, yes!' he said. 'I am starving for greasy, salty ham slices or something like that, like after the time I gave blood.'

Cauda smiled knowingly and from somewhere she picked up a very alien looking knife with a very straight blade, perhaps the same one in the bikini shots. The handle had many indented alien symbols and looked very worn. She put it to her chest between her breasts and winced as she cut an alien symbol very slightly into the surface of the skin. She oozed turquoise blood.

'Eat me,' she ordered, pressing her chest into his mouth.

He did. Her turquoise blood was salty and satisfying with an olive taste. He thought about the old stories of Cuban gigolo-tango dancers that his great-grandmother had told and laughed about. They used to bite the lips of American tourist ladies to taste the blood. As Jack drank her, he felt the strength and strangeness of her alien life force becoming part of him: she was very refreshing to devour. As he returned to the living he felt exhilarated, high even. For a twinkling he was thinking in four sided triangles and round squares rather than in words. Cauda Draconis shook and whimpered as he lapped her up, as though a little part of her were dying. Afterwards, Jack looked at his arms, and for a moment felt surprised that he too did not have olive green skin. Then he fell into a nap.

♀ W ♀

When he awoke it was 9.45 pm. He had met Cauda only two hours and fifteen minutes ago. She sat by him on the bed. She was once again dressed in her purple robe with the alien symbols. The dark green lips were pursed above that little green chin and she looked very serious.

'Get dressed and come with me,' she said softly.

She got up and walked out of the bedroom.

Jack put his clothes on and walked out to the living room. The photos of the children at the beach were still on the wall screen. They looked even more uninteresting. Cauda was on the sofa beckoning him to come sit with her. He sat down by her and she put her six fingered hands into his. She looked deeply into his eyes.

'Honey,' she said, kissing his brows with a sweet smelling perfume of sweat, 'I know we have not known each other long, but I have something very important to tell you.'

She looked frightened. Her brows had tightened up and the pupils of her big saucer eyes had contracted to intense little sapphire points.

'What?' he asked.

'It's difficult.'

'Difficult?'

'Very difficult, earthshattering, prepare yourself.'

She sighed and began crying turquoise blue tears. Was this possible? What had he done to make an alien cry?

Cauda looked hard into his eyes. She pulled his hand close into her robe so he could feel her alien heart beat hard in her green chest. Her wound had disappeared. Surprised, he suddenly pulled his hand back to to his neck and felt that the punctures from her teeth had also healed. She very gently pulled his hand back to her heart.

She looked hard into his eyes once again and said, 'Oh honey, O Jack, I'm pregnant.'

She threw her arms around him and sobbed.

'What?!' he yelled.

'I'm pregnant. And don't you dare think I'm going to get an abortion or something like that!'

'But…,' he said.

'Now don't you give me any "But," you're as responsible as I am.'

He paused and thought about it.

Ashamed to have nothing intelligent to say, he blurted, 'Okay, Okay, what can we do?'

Jack could not believe that this was happening. He suddenly realised that this was a successful hook up and that he owed Out of this World Dating some serious cash.

'What do you mean by "What can we do?" said Cauda angrily through her little green pout. 'I am not about to have the whole galaxy think that my child is without a father. I want to get married.'

'Married!?' he screamed.

Then with silly laughter he said, 'But I don't even have a ring for you.'

'That's all right,' she said, 'I brought them myself.'

From somewhere in the robe she brought out two small transparent rings from a small box made of some translucent and glowing material.

'These rings have been cut from the same flawless diamond mined from the depths of the dwarf planet Pluto. Now, I want you to propose.'

What could he say? She bared her teeth threateningly and hissed. He remembered her great strength as she had pushed his neck into the pillow and sucked the life out of him. He swallowed deeply, heart pounding.

'Cauda Draconis,' he said stiffly, 'will you…'

'No!' she yelped. 'Not like that. Get down on your knees, earth man, like in the old movies and beg me!'

Her iron grip twisted his arm painfully and forced him to the floor before her knees.

'Now beg, earthling! And make it romantic!'

He got up on one knee, took her left hand in his, looked straight into her wide watering turquoise eyes, swallowed hard and pleaded.

'Cauda Draconis, I love you. You are the only woman for me in the whole cosmos. I am begging. Will you marry me?'

She smiled the biggest smile through her dark green lips, showing once again those threatening canine teeth, much longer and hungrier than they had seemed before. Her blue tears had suddenly evaporated.

'Of course, honey!'

He clumsily hesitated as he did not know which of her six lovely green fingers to slip the engagement ring onto. Cauda saw his difficulty.

'Third finger from the left, my delicious pet. It has an artery that comes right from the heart. We shall open it next time you feed.'

He slipped the glowing diamond onto her long green finger.

Suddenly she lifted him from the floor and with one hand held him above her in the air to demonstrate her Herculean strength. She pulled him close into her breast and gave him a long loving kiss shoving her snakelike and turquoise tongue so deep into his throat that he could feel her greedily tasting his tonsils. Despite the strangeness of the last two and a half hours, Jack was deeply in love.

She slipped her serpent tongue out from his throat and again started talking ever so quickly and enthusiastically, otherworldly even, as she wrapped her serpentine limbs about him so that he could not move.

'Our beautiful child will be a girl. I want to call her Stella, Stella Draconis, Dragon's Star, from both our names, sweetheart. She will have an IQ four times the average of you humans. Her skin will be as green as mine and the blood as red as yours. Also, she will have a certain ability to perceive phenomena which you humans are unaware of. Like I said, don't even ask. You can't explain the differential calculus to a dog. Feel the bump in my stomach, she is already kicking.'

She pulled his hand to her swelling belly so that he jumped as he felt his daughter squirm within her.

'Within a mere five thousand years the genes will have spread through your species and the human race shall be no more. There will be in its place a beautiful hybrid race made of the DNA of both our kinds. I want to call the new species Homo Herculensis. You are Adam and I am Eve. Their destiny will be to seed this sector of the galaxy. They will bring the glow of life to the desert of lifeless orbs that circle the nearby stars. Wait a moment, please.'

Cauda let Jack go so he could breathe. She produced a small device not unlike a mobile phone, and said into it, 'Invasion complete, species under assimilation.'

She put the 'phone' away in her purple robe and smiled, 'I said that in your language, just to let you know. The human race has come to an end. Now about the wedding, I've picked out the dress.'

Cauda pulled out a bridal catalogue from her robe, opened it, and pointed to a dress she obviously admired.

She continued talking at light speed. There was no 'beating around the bush' with this girl.

'I picked up this catalogue in town before I parked my saucer in your driveway. You should have seen the sales girls jump at the sight of me as I ran in and out of the shop.'

She laughed and continued, 'The wedding will be here tomorrow at dawn at the point of first contact. I may be naughty, but I like this low cut white wedding dress without shoulders. I want all your earthling friends and relatives, your mother even, to see as much of my beautiful green flesh and cleavage as possible. They will "turn green with envy," as your English expression has it, at the beauty of your bride. Oh, and I want the honeymoon to be on Mars. The low gravity sex will be out of this world. You'll love the view. Phobos is such a beautiful moon as it sets. I've had a wonderful chalet built for us in the red sands of the slope of Mons Olympus, it looks just like one of those fairy tale castles built by crazy King Ludwig II of Bavaria.'

Tonight had obviously been planned well in advance.

Jack ran his hand through Cauda's lovely turquoise blue hair and said, 'Just one problem, honey. Don't you think that the governments of this world will destroy you? Even take military action against you? I mean, after all, you didn't come here with their permission. You are an illegal alien.'

He didn't believe that last sentence had come out of his mouth.

'Just let them try,' she said.

She snapped her green fingers and the wall-sized monitor screen changed to a view of the United Nations building in New York. She laughed and again snapped her fingers. The United Nations building disappeared in an explosion of flame and lightening.

'Just let them try. No child of mine is going to grow up on a planet of governments run by over-privileged oligarchs and dictators making deals with fanatic religious militias. You humans will just have to change the way you do everything.'

She laughed and kissed him again slipping her turquoise blue serpent-tongue past his tonsils and deeply into his thorax so that he could not speak as she tasted him for two.

And they lived happily ever after.

The End

About the Author

Born in England in 1964 c.e, Stewart Black began his rock'n'roll career early, arriving with the first wave of British Invasion bands in 1966 c.e. He grew up in Montréal and Toronto and co-founded punk legends Blibber and the Rat Crushers, The Jolly Tambourine Man and Mike Marley. By 1984 Stewart realized that it was time to die like Sid Vicious or Brat X or to move on. After achieving a whack of degrees in teaching and classical languages *cum laude*, an eleven-year stint teaching English in Japan, and four years as the foremost preparatory school teacher and examiner of Latin in Kenya, East Africa, he returned to his native England where he currently translates nineteenth century French Masonic texts into English and flogs Latin and Greek into rich kids.

Blibber and the Rat Crushers, live at the Turning Point Club, Toronto, circa 1982 c.e. Centre: the author, Stewart Black at seventeen, singer and lead guitar. He is failing to look like the Clash despite oversized collar. Left, Evan "Blibber" Taylor, bass guitar. On drums, incomparable genius, founding member of Toronto punk legends Doomed Youth and The Remains, co-writer of all time favourite Blibber classic, Mommy's in the Mafia, the one, the only Steve Cameron. Photo by Sharny Nicoloff (Sharon Cameron), sister of aforementioned legend Steve Cameron, founder of Toronto's Legendary Diabolics, lead guitar and founding member of surf rock legends, Mark Malibu and the Wasagas as well as cellist extraordinaire.